Amazement

Amazement

GERRY HUERTH

LitPrime Solutions
21250 Hawthorne Blvd
Suite 500, Torrance, CA 90503
www.litprime.com
Phone: 1-800-981-9893

Published by LitPrime Solutions   06/26/2023

ISBN: 979-8-88703-259-7(sc)
ISBN: 979-8-88703-260-3(e)

Library of Congress Control Number: 2023910118

Contents

Chapter 1

A single bird decided it was time and woke the whole chattering sky. The morning commotion sifted through the window screen and stirred a bedroom filled with the smell of boys who wrestle with their sheets on warm nights. Chris's nine year old body startled awake. His head and shoulders popped up setting the bed into a creaking sing song. His younger brother Francis, curled on the other side of the bed, opened his eyes to see his brother silhouetted by the private light that glows just before sunrise. The birds still had this Saturday morning to themselves.

Francis quickly squeezed his eyes into negligible slits, a spy trick he had taught himself a couple of years earlier so that people couldn't tell that he was watching them.

Chris lay there, propped up by his elbows absolutely motionless long after the bed quieted. Finally, the coast clear, he sat up in his tangled sheets. Francis knew that it was safe to open his eyes now. He sat up silently echoing Chris's position. Their oldest brother

Dick, who by virtue of age got to sleep in a separate bed, remained undisturbed in restless dreams.

The Secret Saturday Morning began, a moment stolen from a drowsy bed untroubled with past or future, the half light transforming the world into a place safe for a child's hope. Like synchronized swimmers the brothers crawled out of different sides of their bed and dressed with the solemn determination of childhood. In a flourish of excitement they finished tying their tennis shoes and stood up with simultaneous satisfaction. Chris took the lead as they filed out of the bedroom and into the living room and kitchen. Careful not to slam the screen door, they left the house behind; parents and brother momentarily covered with the safety of sleep.

Once on the street the two walked side by side; Francis occasionally having to sneak in an extra step or two. Chris's face frozen with intensity led them past houses, gray windowed and sightless.

Two blocks beyond their home Chris's pace picked up. Excitement burned through his solemn face. As the first rays of Saturday sun shot horizontally, splattering light against trees and houses, the brothers broke into a run until breathless, they reached the lip of a large sand pit dug against the side of a hill. The loose beige walls were already gathering the warmth of morning as the brothers stopped to reconnoiter. Chris took the lead again as they singly waded down the soft, sloping walls leaving sifting dimples to briefly mark their passage. Finally wide eyed they reached the limestone scattered bottom. Only the drowsy sound of barking distant dogs reminded them of the world beyond this moment.

With urgent purpose the brothers set out in different directions on the look out for pieces of shattered limestone that littered the floor of the quarry like broken plates. Each boy bent down picking up the cool, flat rocks, eyes and fingers searching for fossils encoded with messages from a life that dawned before their concerns. Chris, more driven, found the first precious fragment and fiercely traced the elaborate surface with his fingers. He wildly motioned Francis to come over and place his ear against the powdery surface. Perhaps Francis could hear what Chris couldn't feel.

A little nervously Francis complied. Feeling the cool surface against his cheek for a moment, just for a moment he thought he heard something perhaps some softly whispered answer. Just then the jarring sound of a souped up car on the street above, shattered the possibilities of silence leaving two young boys holding a dull, dead rock.

The bustle of the other Saturday morning began.

Francis understood first and cautiously returned the rock to the sandy floor, his eyes glancing from side to side as if computing strategies for the day ahead. Chris's more earnest face set hard, covering over his inside fire with the innocence of despair.

No longer in sync with his brother's dragging step, Francis took the lead up the shallow end of the pit. He had things to do.

Chapter 2

Well it was too late to do anything about it now; he had things to do and would just have to live with the carroty color of his once gray now unfortunately hennaed hair. As his tight jeans constrained his middle aged bulges with valiant but chaffing determination, Francis took a deep breath and plunged through those swinging doors into the explosion of music.

He picked his way through the chaos of shadowy forms being pounded by the persistent beat and maneuvered his way to the bar around which sat mute, temporary figures. Reluctant to intrude on their disappointment he bought a beer and walked over to a dark wall against which he stationed himself. Once again he waited unable to meet that special man, or for that matter even make eye contact with any of the males in the shadowy line who expectantly almost solemnly filed around the dimly lit gay bar.

Eyes spied out from that line only willing to reveal themselves to someone attractive enough to offset the dangers of exposure. Where hope yet again prevailed over the hazards of fending off unattractive admirers, glances shot out like beacons. The older Francis became, the less those eyes sought his. His periodic maneuvers for attention failed to stop the narrowing quarantine of age.

His own powers as a spy though, were not comprehensive enough to prevent some natural friendliness from showing through his increasingly threadbare gay bar act. He was leaning against that dark wall on the right side of the bar, opposite the spotlighted picture of a muscled cowboy dressed in only holster and gun. Francis stood caught in some unexpected eddy that interrupted the urgency of his own search and momentarily spun his thoughts around his father, his father's recent death. Softer chords of memory filtered through the pounding beat that filled the bar.

A face broke through the male procession looming inches away from Francis.

"Hey man, how are you today?"

"Oh pretty good I guess. It's been a nice day."

"Why haven't I seen you around here before?"

"I come here sometimes." As Francis became more aware of the obvious interest, anticipation diminished his language skills.

"What's a good looking guy like you doing standing here all alone?"

For a moment Francis stood stumped. When nervous he had a disconcerting penchant for the literal; in this case trying to solve the problem of the question instead of just dancing along. The best he could do was to smile beseechingly.

His admirer who was beginning to feel uncomfortable with Francis' lack of bar fluency, decided with some misgivings to persist. The stranger's face pressed even closer establishing territorial mastery. Francis could feel the warm beery moisture of his breath.

"You look hot tonight man."

Indeed Francis suddenly realized how hot the room actually was and nodded.

Finally with emphatic, coded significance the suitor queried, "What do you like to DO, man, what do you like to DO?"

It took Francis a minute to squeeze through his tightening hope. Finally understanding the question and even better having an answer he responded with relief, "I really like to grow house plants and reading; what about you?"

The whitened mask flashed confusion then anger; those interested eyes hooded. "Are you nuts man? I asked what you like to DO!" He started to reach toward his crotch then threw the gesture away with a flick of his wrist.

Like a sentence pronounced, the vague form rejoined the procession.

Francis finished his beer. Sly relief animated his disappointment as if a strategy hidden even from himself had once again succeeded.

He left the bar; the swinging door sealed off the music, smoke, and those searching eyes not wanting to be seen by Francis.

The air rushed around him sharp and clear--even for downtown. It had been an aborted spring. March had shown much promise, snow melting into cold rivers, soil starting to absorb the promised moisture. Then vindictively after some sort of misunderstanding the weather changed its mind and struck with icy ferocity. April 1, sidewalks rang frozen under hurried foot steps. Dirty snow fitfully collected against curbs. People huddled resentfully in their spring jackets. But to Francis the unexpected delay was a relief; spring taunted him with possibilities.

Was it the newly frustrated romance or the gaping hole that had recently replaced his father? Francis felt more than his usual spring anxiety as if something even more disturbing were looming, making demands on him.

He remembered that look on his mother's face yesterday as she had stood guarding the small suburban refuge where she and Chris still lived. With intense cheeriness she had told Francis about the new ceramics class that she was taking. They had smiled at each other blankly. How well she was doing after her recent loss.

When they had not been able to maintain the high spirits any longer, by the unstated mutual consent of compassion, he had decided to leave. They had hugged, warm bodies pressing momentary relief out of the storm of change.

"Well mom, I'll see you next week. The ceramics class sure sounds like fun."

"You know we old gals need to keep busy!" She paused obliquely, "I'm glad you came."

As if covering over some slip, a little too casually she ushered him out of the door watching him walk down the block he had left once as a child.

A couple of houses down Francis turned with quiet suddenness and spied her standing in the doorway, the desolation ringing in her face. It wasn't until that stolen moment that he understood how much she, how much he, missed that embarrassed man, his father.

Poked to attention by the sharp wind Francis returned to his flight from the bar just in time to catch that yellow bubble of a bus as it slowed, stopped, and opened its accordion doors for him. He sat with people like himself who apologetically needed public transportation. The Prosperous Others zoomed by at their private velocities, radios playing; leaving old women, men out of work, children, and Francis perched on those more common seats at the mercy of frequent stops.

With the discipline learned in a six week adult education class on meditation, entitled "You Too Can Relax and Become a Winner," Francis valiantly attempted to empty his taut mind into repeating breaths. Otherwise the forty five minute ride from the bar punctuated with random stops would have outraged his private sense of time, after all he had things to do.

Unfortunately his stubborn mind soon refused the fitful discipline, intent on establishing its own order. As Frances' face went blank his mind pictured a younger self with mom, dad, Chris, and Dick on Sunday night; all five of them flickering in the dark living room intent on that new miracle, 1950's television. Even the new pole lamp stood darkly ignored next to the sofa. Only Dick as usual was squirming in and out of the bathroom with the urgency of precocious puberty.

Between Ed Sullivan and the Wonderful World of Disney one of those Charlie Tuna commercials flashed on. Each tuna advertising episode had a lone cartoon character, Charlie Tuna. As usual finny Charlie was arduously attempting to demonstrate good taste: playing a violin, reading Shakespeare, studying opera, or anything that passed for high culture in those post-World War II years.

In spite of Charlie's obviously earnest attempts, a cartoon hook was lowered by the unsympathetic folks at Star Kist, "Sorry Charlie, Star Kist likes tuna that tastes good."

As the silent, yellow bus smoothly and successfully rolled through yet another green light, Chris saw that hook lowering ominously into his increasingly peculiar middle age. He couldn't quite make out that hooked sign except that it started with, "Sorry Francis..."

Finally recognizing his own street corner he pulled

the cord. This time the accordion doors released him into the cold night.

The sound of his own key unlocking the door broke his spell. He stepped into the reassuringly enclosed environment of his own apartment, flicking on the light switch. His plants mutely greeted him as they clustered around their windows with silent but persistent longing. Spring was the time of year in which he liked nothing more than to simply sleep; with a wistful smile, silently, ceremoniously, shedding his clothes, climbing into the gently rasping sheets, yes, this is enough.

His pilgrimage to bed was unceremoniously interrupted by the blinking red light of his answering machine. On-off, on-off, on-off. The invitation of a telephone message intruded, a tiny violation signaling someone else's need. He reached over and clicked on the recording.

"Hi, Francis, this is your brother Chris. Do you want to go out for breakfast Saturday morning? Why don't you give me a call? Ok? Frances? See you."

Francis stared at his reflection on the shiny black slate of the window. He grimaced at his audience in coy complaint. "Oh yeah, it's Friday night. You'd think Chris would just come over on Saturday morning. Nooooo, not Chris, he's got to leave the same message every Friday evening; the exact same message as if it's some brilliant new plan. We've only been doing this for…years."

He paused and turned away from his reflection in the window and whispered, "Years."

Looking around the room, nodding slowly at the quiet green witnesses around him, he lowered his body onto the bed and stared straight up at the ceiling as if it were a sky. "Back then I thought I could escape."

His face glimmered in curiosity as he slipped into the maze of memory. The fascination of story telling began budding through his customary reluctance; perhaps through that very hole his father had left behind. He whispered to himself, "Back then…"

He shook his head wondering how many selves ago he still had, had that hope. He closed his eyes, not to sleep or even concentrate; simply to finally listen to those distant voices telling old stories of adventure and sorrow.

Now caught in the web of something like wonder he slowly nodded his head, "Yeah, that was the year I went to the seminary."

Chapter 3

No one really asked me why I was going. People just supposed. I was in the eight grade, the nuns liked me, and I wasn't very good at sports. Besides my parents had named me Francis. I wasn't a Frank, like I said before, I didn't do very well at sports. I didn't want people to call me Frannie either. Who knows what the boys in my class would do with that name? So I'm stuck with Francis.

A lot of the girls and boys in my eight grade class had already started making out at parties. I didn't mind not being invited to a lot of the parties. Making out just wasn't for me. I was invited to Tim's party though. I spent time with him. He wanted me to teach him how to throw a ball like a boy; I guess I had managed to do that. Tim was someone I could be around so that I wasn't all alone on the playground.

I am very careful never to look like I am alone; people especially boys would think that there is something wrong with a kid who stands there alone. My older brother Chris didn't have anyone to stand around with during recess, and I saw what happened to him.

But back to Tim's party. It was actually his mother's idea. He got invited to fewer parties than I did. So he and his mother invited all the popular kids in class and me too. That party seemed just about the most important thing that ever happened in that home; I never saw so much pop, potato chips, and potato chip dip in one place. That place was the basement, and no adults could come down.

I got there first, and then all the kids who didn't talk to to me very much, started coming. Those popular boys all played sports. Even when they weren't actually on a team together they talked in this loud way, like they were still on some court together. Anybody who wasn't exactly like them was on the other team. Let me tell you sports can be pretty hard if you are on the other team. You see the other team has to loose, has to be really slaughtered. I knew I was on the other team when I watched Chris get slaughtered. I knew that I didn't want that to happen to me. So I learned this trick about becoming invisible. I was smart enough not to look stupid, and nice enough not to get anybody mad. I smiled a lot, although not too much.

The boys brought their pretty girl friends too. The girls weren't so bad; they just hung around those boys in this funny way, like they were nothing if the boys didn't see them. Of course there were unpopular girls too, the ones who weren't pretty. They weren't invited to Tim's or anybody's parties. They didn't have to try to be invisible; they just were. I think Tim's mother wanted him to be one of those popular kids. She didn't know it was a lost cause. I knew it was, and not just for Tim.

There we were twenty kids in the basement with more pop and potato chips than most stores have. I was very nice, trying not to get into anybody's way, making sure the bowls of potato chips were full, and that there was plenty of fast music on the record player. It's not that I was dancing or anything like that, I just wanted the music to stay fast. Besides everybody thought that I would go to the seminary when I got out of eighth grade.

Then as if it were all planned, Tim put on some very slow music and turned the lights out. This was the part that everyone else was waiting for except me. After a while when I got used to the dark, I could see shadowy, spooky figures coming together. I knew that I could finally stop smiling. The music even seemed kind of peaceful. Occasionally the floor above us would gently creak as the Tim's father would get up to turn the TV channel.

But then a girl named Nancy asked me to dance. She didn't quite fit in either. She was too smart, and she didn't hide it well enough. She was kind of pretty. Pretty enough to be invited to most parties, but she didn't fit with any boy very well. She walked a little different than the really pretty girls. She stood on two feet instead of always trying to lean on a boy. Most of the other girls tried to act stupid in class, but she still asked questions. I guess she wanted to know about things.

She walked up to me in the dark and touched me on the shoulder. "Francis, do you want to dance?" I smiled until I realized that it was so dark that she couldn't see my face. "Sure Nancy," I said.

Our bodies came together in the dark. I don't remember ever having been up front so close to anybody before. It felt a little funny her pressing against me like that, but she was quite a bit shorter, and I liked her a little.

Everything was going okay as we kind of shuffled in the dark until she said, "What do you think about making out?" Now maybe to some of the other boys this would have been good news; it wasn't to me. I was glad it was dark because maybe she wouldn't see how scared I was, scared that she would figure out that I was not the kind of boy who was attracted to girls.

I tried to sound very kind but serious, the way the priests do. "It's impure to make out, Nancy. It's a sin. We shouldn't do it." I tried not to sound angry or anything, but just very sure of what people were supposed to do.

She was very quiet for a while; her body stopped going back and forth. I didn't know what she was thinking, but felt very relieved that I had a pretty good reason for not making out. She stopped pushing at me. And then she said, "You're such a good boy Francis. You're so nice." I could see the way her head was bent down she was waiting for something, like me to forgive her and give her a penance for having wanted to do something impure. She just stood there in the dark as if there was something wrong with her not me.

Like I said I was relieved, but I felt funny inside about what I told her. It wasn't just that I didn't give her what she wanted, but I gave her all the wrong reasons, and if she's anything like me…I suppose no one is really like me.

Things really aren't that simple; definitely not for me. Sure there's some things that are easy and fun, like building rafts on the pond with Chris and Dick. Dick is my oldest brother. I have two of them. But a lot of the time it's like being a spy running across a field where there are bombs buried underneath, just waiting to be stepped on. BAM! I'm splattered to smithereens. If someone nice like Nancy asks me a question I don't even think about letting her know what's going on. I never know when the bomb will go off.

I'm doing OK in eight grade, getting B's mostly. I don't think I'm really smart though. I've seen a few kids, not always the ones who get good grades, who seem like they really want to understand things. They don't look like they are so afraid. I wonder sometimes what it would feel like to want to figure things out instead of just walking very, very carefully. There's something going on inside them that seems even more mysterious than the Mass I have to go to everyday at the Catholic school I go to.

With me though, I have learned to avoid anything that is serious when I talk to people, to not let on how things really are, to not be too curious. Curiosity is mostly bad news. The outside of things are what's really important. I want to get good grades. It makes things feel safer. It makes me feel special too. Even though I'm not good at sports or that smart, I can still feel like I'm better than somebody else. It's very important to feel like you're better than someone else; it's easier to be a spy that way.

Which brings me back to the first part, about everybody supposing I would go to the seminary. I supposed so too. It was a place that seemed safe for someone like me. For the last couple of years priests from different religious orders have come by to speak to my class, like army recruiters. They're usually young and handsome and seem like really glamorous uncles. They come in, look you straight in the eye and smile as if they recognize something inside you that is wonderful just like them. Then they pass out pamphlets that show new buildings and boys smiling while they study or play sports. When the boys in these pictures are praying they almost look like saints. I just know they don't have to make out with girls. I know that I can smile and look good like the best of them.

I suppose I am kind of religious. Because I go to a Catholic school, I have to go to Mass in the morning before class. When I pray at Mass especially after communion, I feel safe almost holy. Once in a while if I've been kneeling for along time and it's hot and I've skipped breakfast; everything gets sort of wavy and out of focus like something religiously important is going to happen to me.

In spite of all that, I'm very concerned about hell. I know something inside me is bad, something hidden most of the time. Last year the parish priest called all the seventh grade boys out of class and into his rectory. We all knew it must be something pretty important. He had this funny look on his face like he was a little sick to his stomach or something. Then he explained about impure thoughts, that they're when a movie goes on in your head, except naked people are in this movie. If you don't stop this movie playing right away you commit what's called a mortal sin. This means you go to hell if you die before you confess it to a priest. Hell is like another movie, a non-stop Dracula movie in which horrible things happen over and over again forever. If this horrible punishment happens to you for having impure thoughts, you can imagine what happens if you actually do something dirty with yourself or someone else, especially if it's with another boy. The priest didn't go into details about specifically forbidden things that we might do; maybe he didn't want to start any movies going on in our heads. By the end of his talk though, he looked at us sadly as if we might be lost causes. As we left he rushed upstairs, like he had to go to the bathroom or something.

Once I did check out this book from the library.

It was about a man named Ulysses, and it had some pictures. About midway through the book there was a picture of Ulysses without a shirt on. A hungry looking woman named Circe was grasping for him. My world split open. I wanted to reach for him too, but unlike Circe I could only take very fast, accidental glances. Sometimes when I am walking home I would start thinking about Ulysses, so I would start singing hymns at the top of my voice. I've gotten pretty good about turning off the movies. After all it would be pretty hard to confess an impure thought. You get in a confessional with other kids waiting just outside. There's this priest behind a screen whom you recognize and who probably recognizes you. You tell him about having impure thoughts. What happens if he asks for details? Some do. I make it easier on myself; I just won't have impure thoughts.

I have enough to deal with being a sissy. I play some sports so I don't look too strange. I have even learned like I said before, to throw like a boy. The making out stuff is beyond me though. That's where the seminary comes in.

A particularly nice priest came to talk with us in class. He said that if any of us were interested we could see another even more important priest downtown St. Paul. Now it's midway through my eighth grade and I know I need to do something pretty quick. This was after Tim's party. I told my mother that I wanted to see the priest in Minneapolis.

The first thing I knew, there I was sitting in a

rectory slightly behind my mother. We both were sitting in a large room with polished stone floors, facing an important looking gray priest sitting behind a huge desk. In the distance I heard sounds in the rectory kitchen and smelled delicious food. A woman a little older than the priest stepped into the room and spoke in serious whispery voice, "Father when would you like me to serve you lunch?" The gray priest looked kind of irritated, but then answered her in that way that priests do when they are getting ready to forgive you, almost like he actually was her father. "Mary, I'll be ready in forty minutes." He smiles; she smiles. I can notice all of this because I'm hiding behind my mother. I think we were both impressed by someone who lives in such a place and has people around who take care of him. I was relieved, hiding behind my mother's back, that I didn't have to do too much. She knows how to handle things.

I said I was hiding behind my mother because that's how it must have looked. It was more complicated than that. Mom and I didn't really talk about it, but somehow she knew that I had to leave home. We were always like that. She was a window or this time a door out into the world for me. She was my first memory. I'm not sure how old I was, but I must have been pretty young because my mother seemed so much taller than me that her head kind of disappeared in a foggy mist way up there. My hand rested in hers. We were outside in the gray and cold, standing together looking up a long sidewalk to a building made of glass that was filled with the color green. She said, "That's a green house. There are flowers in there the whole year."

I said, "What about winter, mommy?"

She looked down at me from way up there. "It's always warm in the green house, Francis. The flowers are safe."

I felt her smile and squeezed her hand. I smiled too just thinking about a place where there are plants, all the time, safe, just like heaven.

When I was a little older but way before I saw the gray priest in Minneapolis, I remember her again but this time it was strange. I woke up one night and there in the yellow lighted doorway was this angry woman-monster, hair standing up on end shooting out sparks. I'm still not sure if that was mom or just a dream. But I do think she may have some spy parts about her too.

On the way home from visiting the gray priest my mom very seriously asked me, "Is this the seminary that you want to go to?" We didn't have to talk about whether I should go. I said "Yes."

She nodded. We both knew I needed a place to grow up in. Neither of us had traveled much, so it was not so important whether the seminary was in St. Cloud, Minnesota or Philadelphia, Pennsylvania. That's where the priest said Mary Valley was. I liked the name. It sounded peaceful.

The rest of my eight grade year went by all right. I told the nuns and the other kids what I was doing. The nuns started treating me like I was some one special, and none of the girls asked me to make out. Things were settled. I like having things that way.

Things never seemed settled at home. I have two older brothers. Dick is the oldest, three years older than me. We're always at opposite ends of what ever goes on. He seems to like things to be very confused. I like things to go smoothly as can be. My brother Chris is two years older. We used to like to go exploring when we were kids. He's being beaten up regularly on the bus to junior high school. He's taller than me, smarter, curious even. Other kids want to hurt him. Some mornings I wake up and even though I am pretending to sleep, I watch him to try to figure out what it is that makes kids want to hurt him. Maybe I could warn him, or at least I can be careful that I don't do what he does. For sure, he never learned how to be a spy.

When Chris and I were at Uncle Bob's and Aunt Jean's house for a picnic and as usual we didn't know what to say to our pretty, popular cousins, I could see that Chris was having even a harder time than me. I tried to explain to him when we walked out back. "Chris you got to just try to smile like everything is all right. People like you better that way."

He looked at me in that funny way of his, like he was broken hearted that people didn't like him the way he was. He didn't look angry just sad and confused the way he did when he tried to figure things out in the morning. He just looked at me that way, and I knew it was a hopeless cause. I had no way to explain to him that pretending makes things safer. I admire him, but I think that he is headed towards trouble.

Or maybe trouble is already here. Like the time during a grade school festival in my sixth grade. All the parents would set up booths in the gym. Parents in some booths sold raffle tickets, and others sold hot dogs or pop. A few booths sold white elephants, although I didn't see anything nearly big enough to look like that. I guess adults need to have fun too.

I was having a pretty good time helping to sell hot dogs when Tim comes running up to me and says that some boys have Chris up on the school roof. I knew that Chris had bought a stack of used comic books at the festival and that they were his treasure. I ran up the stairs onto the roof to see a few older boys holding Chris. He was trying break loose from them. His face looked wild. The rest of boys were tearing up those comics and laughing. The colored pages flew away in the wind like frightened birds. That's when I knew for sure I was a spy, because I just watched those frightened birds from a distance.

Then it was all over. I'm not even sure Chris knew I saw what happened, but it became another one of the reasons I had to go.

Bud McCoy is another reason. Bud lived next door. Some of the older boys used to call me half girl. I didn't like it especially since I thought it was true, but it was just words. Bud was real, more real than words. Somehow he found me out and surprised me like an explosion.

Bud was a big guy who was in high school. I was in kindergarten. After lunch one summer afternoon I went outside. I used to love walking in the fields alone, turning over rocks looking for ant colonies. Those ants would move around so orderly like they knew exactly what they were supposed to do. Well, Bud came up to me and asked real kindly, "Francis, do you want to go for a walk in the fields with me?" Even though Bud had seemed a little tough, I felt real pleased that someone that old wanted to be friends with me. I said yes. We walked into the fields, me feeling proud to be with a big guy. I remember the warm sun in the tall grass. It kind of made a crinkling sound when we walked through it.

The next thing I remember, I'm sitting on the ground by my favorite tree. I know Bud is right next to me, but it's like a nightmare where you know some terrible monster is coming, but you can't see him. I'm really scared, but I'm watching myself too almost like I am on the outside. Maybe that's how I learned how to watch Chris. Anyway I see that I can't stop crying.

I here Bud say, "Now it's your turn, you put your finger in my ass!" Most nightmares end before I see the monster, but this time it was different. Like I said before I was watching myself from the outside, but when I turned toward him I was back in my face again and I was looking out. Tears were falling so fast that it was almost like looking out of a car into a car wash, every thing all wet and blurry. For just a flash I saw his naked, smelly butt, and then everything seemed to tear into pieces. I don't know what happened right after that except that even now I don't like any of the smells that come from down below and I never, never will put anything of mine into anybody's butt.

It was late afternoon when he finished with me. It's not that I remember time going by because I just remember little flashes. But I know it was late afternoon because the sun wasn't very bright when I walked out of the fields with him, and I was afraid I would be late for supper. I didn't hear the grass crinkle or anything; I just didn't want to be late because my parents might find out what happened.

Bud had his belt doubled up in one hand and he slapped it against his other hand, "If you tell anybody about this, you'll be whipped." I didn't know if he meant other people will whip me if they find out, or he will. Either way sounded real bad. Besides, my mom and dad seemed pretty happy in that neighborhood; I didn't want to mess that up for them. Ever after though, I felt sick to my stomach whenever I saw Bud and I didn't like to go into the fields anymore.

Two years after this I had my first confession. I knew I had to confess what happened to me because I had done something terrible with Bud. I was very nervous but relieved to be able to tell somebody. Once in the confessional I blurted the story out almost right away. The priest was kind of impatient, but he forgave me. I remember walking home and feeling so clean. That confession was the first time I tried to stop being a spy. Maybe that's part of the reason I wanted to be a priest. It helped me, what that priest did. Besides being a priest is the most glamorous thing a boy like me who doesn't like sports can be.

Before the trip to Mary Valley I didn't really think about it a lot. Things were just done almost like magic, like buying a bus ticket, finding a suitcase, packing clothes, and getting instructions for how to find my way form my home in West St. Paul to Philadelphia and then to Mary Valley. I think mom probably figured out a lot of it. My dad is nervous and a little embarrassed. In the weeks before the trip once in a while I'd catch him looking at me in a far off way. We never did talk too much.

I think he was sad I was going away, like it was his fault. He thought a lot of things were his fault. I wished I could tell him it's not because of him that I'm leaving, but the way that the future seems like terrible trouble and I don't want to wait for it to happen to me here.

It's funny how really big changes, even if you know they're going to happen, sneak up on you. It's just that time disappears. One morning in early September I got up and I'm leaving. I say goodbye to mom, we hug. She looks determined but kind of soft. It makes leaving easier that she doesn't cry. My dad seems more confused, more helpless than me. After all I know what's going on. He and I walk in slow motion to the car dragging our feet to slow things down even more. Inside we sit. The car is still for the longest time like when there is interference on the television. The movie stops and you don't really know if it will start again. My dad and I are caught in this time between movies. We don't say anything, but we sit side by side, waiting. Then the engine starts and breaks the embarrassment before it becomes tender. I sit looking out the window as the movie outside goes by and my dad is next to me. I smell the apple smell of his tobacco and it smells so good to me that I want to forget about it. I'm going away. I look out of the window again at the movie, and I pretend that I don't notice when he looks at me.

The car stops. We need to do things now. He steps out. I step out. He goes back and opens the trunk. I make sure I have my ticket in my pocket. He carries the big, light blue suitcase. I open the big glass door. We both step into the bus terminal that is so full of strange sounds that kind of echo. My dad takes the lead with the big blue suite case now.

We wait silently while a deep male voice coming from nowhere and everywhere recites over the loud speaker a litany of city names ending with, "To Chicago and points east, now boarding on track 8." I'm a little bit outside of myself again. Part of me is in the bus terminal and part of me is under water watching everything. I finally look away from the blue suite case to dad. He looks like he doesn't know what to do next. I think he knows better than to ask me if I'll be all right. I'm in the car wash again, but I'm not struggling this time. I know it's best to go. We walk out a door behind a line of people into this huge garage that smells like gasoline. My dad hands my suitcase to the bus driver who sticks it in a big compartment under the bus with a bunch of other suitcases. I wonder if I'll ever get it back again.

I walk into the shadowy bus; it has a special smell like a closet that has dirty clothes in it. It's quiet in here like the inside of a bubble or at least how it must be like in the inside of a bubble. I crawl into a seat that is much taller than I am and it feel all right except I'm still wondering if I will ever get my suite case back. My suite case is all I have left, and if that gets lost; I can't even think about that so I look through the darkened glass windows that make everything seem silent and gray on the other side. I see my father crying; I look away so I don't embarrass him. Besides I have things to worry about now like if this actually is the bus to Chicago and if I actually get to Chicago, how do I find the bus to Philadelphia. And then there's the suite case that I know somebody else is going to take. I sit back into the seat with the funny smell. I am bouncing back and forth between all the things that might go wrong. The bus driver kind of hops on the bus takes one last look at all of us, and sits down in his seat closing the door and ending my life in West St. Paul.

I take one last look at my dad. My eyes are just barely open enough so I can see. Maybe my dad will feel better if he thinks I'm so comfortable I'm falling asleep. The bus starts smoothly moving, hardly making any sound. My dad and everything outside sails away.

Chapter 4

And the next thing I know I'm headed off towards Wisconsin. It's still very quiet in the bus although once and while I hear people talking quietly as if they are in church. The sun is shining but looks a little gray because of the dark windows. It's very silent out there. My family used to go to Tomah, Wisconsin to visit my grandfather. Tomah is about half way to Chicago my dad used to say. When my family went there, it was always pretty noisy. Dick had this way of getting in trouble. Before I knew it I would hear my dad say to my mom, "Can't you keep the boys quiet, Joan?" Chris and I knew that this wasn't really a question and that if we didn't stop right away my mother would turn around with that look in her eyes that meant business. Unfortunately Dick never got the point. Before I would know it, Dick and dad would start arguing, and then mom would argue with both of them and finally settle on dad. By this time I would close my eyes and pretend that I really wasn't part of this family; I was just along for the ride. Chris would just stare and listen like maybe there was something he was supposed to do about it all.

Wisconsin is as far away from home as I have ever been, and even then I wasn't alone. My Grandfather ran away from my grandmother when my dad and his brothers were just boys. My grandmother is an Indian, my father said, although she wouldn't talk about it and seemed real angry if someone mentioned it. She washed dishes and cleaned houses during the Great Depression to keep her boys fed. They lived in a poor Italian neighborhood and sort of fit in there. My father talked how they ate beans and molasses and nothing else.

Funny how I miss Dick, even. At least things wouldn't be so quiet.

What can I say about the trip? It's like falling through a hole in slow motion, and all the time I keep worrying about losing my suite case. I have always worried a lot, but this trip is different. Back at home there was always a commotion going on around me, but I always knew how to get away from it by becoming a spy.

This trip is more like jumping into a swimming pool (something I never really liked), the way for a second you're just kind of hanging there all alone up in the air and no one can stop you from smashing into the water that may be very cold, and it's your decision that set the whole thing in motion. Kind of like with Bud when I said that I would go into the fields with him. I did have more time to think about this trip first though. Not that I really understand what it was all about.

Sitting in this bus is like waiting to smash into the future all alone. Some kids seem to be able to play more, jump off things and laugh about it. They don't seem to know that terrible things happen underwater. I've never laughed very much. You have to believe in nice surprises to laugh. Normally I don't try new things, especially things that are supposed to be fun. Fun leads to mistakes. I hope this trip isn't a mistake.

There are what seem to be a million stops all day at lonely Wisconsin towns. Each stop the sun gets a little dimmer. Each stop I'm afraid that the bus driver will accidentally take my suitcase off. It's easier to worry about losing my suitcase at every stop than to think about Chicago, and how I have to change busses there. The furthest I can imagine is the picture of me getting off this bus. Then it's a blank, except I know I have to do it and that Chicago is big and scary. Once and a while I try to picture a sunny place where smiling boys don't play too many sports, but I only draw a blank that twists my stomach.

I'm so nervous about things, but still I want the trip to go on forever so I don't have step off the bus into Chicago. When the sky is getting gray and shadowy, I see this glow in the sky way ahead. The farms are giving way to houses and then houses to tall buildings with cars speeding between them shining their headlights every which way.

Inside the bus yellow lights turn on. The bus turns

up and down dark streets and then finally goes into a pitch black tunnel. Just when I start wondering if the maybe the bus driver is lost, the bus drives out into this big parking lot way down deep in the earth. So deep you wonder if you can get out. With his back of his head to us the bus driver says, "Chicago, last stop, everybody out."

Everybody else looks like there relieved to be home. I breathe once deeply to prepare myself. I try to remember all the things I need to do. First I need to somehow get my suitcase before somebody else takes it. I have to hold on to my ticket. I have to make sure no one takes my wallet. Most of all I need to somehow find the right bus, the one to Philadelphia.

I am the last person out of the bus and for a moment I stand at the top of the stairs of the bus all the noise and commotion are down below and it's all coming at me. I go down the stairs, and then I'm completely submerged in light and noise. The first specific thing I actually hear is the scrapping sound of the bus driver throwing the luggage onto the cement floor. What if someone already took it? And then I see him grab my big blue suitcase. I holler as loud as I can, trying to get through all that noise, "That's mine! That's mine!"

As my suitcase hits the ground, that big man in the bus uniform looks at me as if he has just woken up. I scramble over to the suitcase. He's next to me now. I need to get it before someone else takes it. His hand is sliding the suitcase towards me and from way up above I hear, "Be careful, there's all sorts down here, watch out for your wallet." I look up for a second at his face. For a tiny second I see him looking at me, and then he goes off to get more suitcases down.

I feel a little better holding on to my suitcase. All around me are tall adults who know exactly where they are going. I start asking everyone I bump into where I catch the bus to Philadelphia. I must look like a ball bouncing back and forth between people, asking questions over and over again, but every time I bounce I get another clue. I use all my skill as a spy to find the right bus. Finally a nice woman shows me where the ticket counter is and the man behind the counter points out a line that I need to stand in. The sign above the door says Philadelphia. I'm still pretty scared, but I feel good about finding the right bus, or at least I hope the sign is right. I start asking questions again just to make sure.

I leave my suitcase with the new bus driver and again walk up the bus steps into the yellow light all around me; the seats are just like the ones on the St. Paul bus, and for a moment my stomach feels all jumpy when I realize I have a family back where I came from and they're all just getting ready for supper.

Supper on Saturday nights is my favorite time, or was my favorite time. Dad isn't so anxious about work and he makes his special fried chicken. First he puts it in the deep fryer and then he bakes it. He says that baking it is the secret. My mother seems pretty happy not to be cooking and she has finished all her housework. Sometimes on Saturday afternoons she even visits girl friends. My parents seem pretty happy with each other on Saturday nights.

Then the bus to Philadelphia is all filled with people. I am very relieved to have a seat. The bus driver jumps into his seat, glances back at the passengers. The bus motor starts rumbling and we once again turn into the black tunnel. It's night in Chicago now.

Even though there are so many people, the bus is still very quiet. All the other passengers look safe and talk with reassuring whispers to each other. A large woman carrying a brown paper bag is sitting next to me. She stares absentmindedly into the night while cracking and eating hard boiled eggs. I think about food for the first time today and grab for the sandwiches my mother made me. Back home my family's talking about what television they'll see tonight. My mother makes popcorn too, with lots of butter.

As I unwrap my sandwiches even that memory falls through a hole.

I have never slept with strangers before. Now it's like no one knows I'm here. I keep my eyes closed. Once and a while I spy at the people around me through slits between my eye lids, but finally I fall asleep. Later I get up to urinate and have to crawl over the woman with the brown paper bag. She's snoring. Even late at night some people are still whispering to each other under domes of light. Everything is dark outside, the motor hums; it's easier now.

I wake up like somebody shook me. The sun is shining on something that must be mountains. They rise almost vertically, like the land is tipped sideways. They're green; trees growing up and down. At the base of some of the mountains are piles of houses that almost look like they slipped down the sides and are making do all crunched together. I'm not so worried about the luggage any more. We stop at a place called Howard Johnson's and I have breakfast alone, another first time for me. Maybe it's the way the morning shines on the green, but for a couple of moments I think somehow this trip might work. I get back on the bus. During that stop the woman with hard boiled eggs disappeared.

This whole day starts in a way that is completely new for me. At first that feels pretty good, but I start thinking I don't know how this day will end. I have all these things to do that I have never done before. I really do like to do things I do over and over again. I'm less likely to make a mistake and get noticed. Even though the sun is still shining I feel a new kind of tiredness that wipes the morning away. I don't care so much about anything now. We pass out of those mountains and things start looking ugly. Everything looks real flat with lots of people and buildings all crowded in on each other. Everything looks so strange. All those houses crowded together look different than the ones in St. Paul. These houses are connected in a row with no yards in between. People sit outside on their steps like they have no place to go.

I try to imagine that seminary I'm going to, but I can't. Knowing the bus trip is just about over I force myself to get real alert. Yesterday I was just afraid all the time. I kept real awake. Today I feel heavy, but still I sit on the edge of my seat so I can figure things out. Philadelphia--I have to find the train station and then catch not just any train but the right one. I've never been on a train before. I need to get on the train to Mary Valley before dark and then find my way from the train stop to the seminary, all the way with the big blue suitcase. The seminary sent me typed instructions, but the words are all about things that I don't know how to do or have never seen before, like a horrible puzzle that doesn't make any sense. The falling into a hole happens again, and the bus is driving through this city that looks even stranger than Chicago. I look at my lap until the bus finally stops and stands still.

At least when I step down the stairs in Philadelphia it's still pretty light. On my spy mission I grab my big blue suitcase and step away from the bus to examine my instructions again for the millionth time. One thing at a time, just keep moving. I'm pretty good at just keeping moving especially if I have instructions in my hand. Even if I don't understand them they give me a sense of purpose, nothing long range, just what's next. I am in Philadelphia in a bus station. I don't have to think about Mary Valley. I start walking in the same direction as everybody else; this isn't so bad. We all go into this huge bus station. Everybody scatters in different directions leaving me not sure who I should follow. So I do what I can do and bounce back and forth between strangers asking questions. People look puzzled and point in different directions. Finally I drag my suitcase in front of a woman sitting on a bench. I show her my directions this time. She doesn't seem at all confused by them and tells me I should step out the main door and stand on the sidewalk until a taxi comes and then just say that I want to go to the train station. And just like she said, I get to the sidewalk and mysteriously a taxi stops. The driver is older than my dad, and inside the taxi smells like an old lunch box, but the man looks at me, reassuring and impatient at the same time; so I settle down in the seat. I begin to look at Philadelphia. It looks so old and fancy and dirty; I don't know what to think. The taxi driver mutters under his breath, "What's a kid like that doing out all alone?" I feel like apologizing, but I know that I'm not a kid anymore. I haven't been for a long time.

I'm let out at the train station and actually figure out where to buy a ticket. Waiting I wander around, the banging sound of passing trains fills my mind. I ask three different people where to catch the train to Mary Valley. They all say the same thing, so it's probably true.

I get on the train and show the conductor my instructions. He says, "Don't worry I'll call your stop off." I still worry he'll forget. It starts sneaking up on me that I'm reaching the end of my trip and try to imagine happy seminarians and happy me; but the late afternoon sun shows messy towns, old gas stations, and buildings too close together, all junky looking too.

I start keeping my focus inside the train because it starts getting dark outside. Every time we stop at a city I look at that man in uniform. He shakes his head again. Finally he calls out "Mary Valley!" He glances at me and nods.

It's a run down old station that looks like it needs paint. One last time I show the conductor my instructions. I guess I hoped that this was the wrong place. He points way in the distance at a spooky old building up on a hill. Besides it's pretty dark outside now.

My body feels dull and heavy as I yank up my suitcase and step off the train. I just stand there and watch the last thing that connected me from where I came from disappear. It's quiet now and I am standing there all alone. I look towards that shadowy building way up that hill. It has kind of towers like something out of a horror movie. It's pretty dark now.

The building is real big at least three stories tall all made of wood with a long sagging porch that hangs off the front. I can just make out a muddy pond at the bottom of the hill. It looks like this used to be country around here before the city crowded all around leaving this building stranded. I walk up the dark winding driveway and hear a few ducks squawking from the dark pond. It's finally night, and I don't feel anything except maybe disappointment. I walk up the wooden steps and knock on the tall door. Everything seems pretty dark and quiet inside. Finally I hear the creaking foot steps of somebody coming from deep inside the building. The door opens, "Who are you?"

"I'm Francis Schmidt. I've come to the seminary. This is Mary Valley isn't it?"

The form in the darkened doorway scans me with irritation. "Ya, you're three days early."

Chapter 5

While the man says his name is Vince, I fall through another hole. Some back part of my mind hears my mother say, "Bill (my father), how could you have done that?" My dad has that look on his face when he has just made a mistake. The first time I remember that look was when I was about three years old. My penis had an infection on it. There was a little pocket of skin underneath the edge of the cap. Lint got in and the skin grew over it. I really don't remember much except my dad driving me in the car. There was something different about the way he looked at me, kind of embarrassed.

Next thing I remember, I'm sitting on the edge of a cold metal table. The doctor says, "This isn't going to hurt." For a second I see my father in the far corner looking at me with that embarrassed look of his. Then I feel a burning pain and everything flashes and shatters. Next thing I remember the nurse is telling me that the doctor has cut out the infection and I need to be more careful how I wash down there.

I don't think I have ever picked up all those fractured pieces of my dad, ever.

Vince stares at me while I'm thinking. Then he says, "I guess it doesn't matter, come with me." He leads me through some shadowy hallways and up some stairs and finally turns on the light of a locker room. "You said your name is Meyers?"

I nod.

He points to a locker, "Unpack here." Then as if announcing a reprieve he says, "There's some supper left." He disappears.

The locker room itself has a long trough like sink with a whole bunch of faucets down the middle. The lockers are gym lockers lining the walls except where tall windows with paint peeling of the frames interrupt them. Just like in a Dracula movie there are no mirrors. The scraping sound of my locker door opening reminds me, I'm in this movie.

I hear voices; Vince is back. He's leading another boy who seems to have come early too, except he doesn't look embarrassed like it's not a big concern to him that he made a mistake. He's kind of short and walks into the locker room like it's already home. He looks me straight in the eye and says," Hi, I'm Johnny Jodell, and I'm from Richland, West Virginia. Who are you?" And then he puts his hand out to me like he really does want to get to know me.

Kind of formally I say, "Glad to meet you Johnny Jodell. My name is Frances Meyers and I'm from

St. Paul." And I shake his hand for a second while I look down.

Then he says hey, "You can call me Johnny. How was your trip?"

"Oh pretty long but not so bad." I look across to him and he's still smiling so I say, "How did you get here?" I'm looking straight at him now.

"I got on a bus from Richland. Yikes that was a long trip. For a while I thought I was going to be on that darn bus forever. Let me tell you I didn't know there were so many towns between Richland and here." He starts laughing. "How did you get here Francis?"

"I came by bus too."

"Woowie! All the way from Minnesota!"

I like how happy he talks, easy, like it comes natural to him. Maybe he doesn't know we made a mistake and got here too early. I try to break it to him gently. "We're early. We came too early. We weren't supposed to be here for three days."

"Well I'll be darned. Maybe we can get a head start getting to know this place."

"You think?"

"I saw a pond just waiting to be explored. Who knows what else is around here."

I smile for the first time in days. There's something nice and easy when two people smile at each other. Even Vince seems friendlier. He not only shows us where to go for supper but promises to take us out on a ride tomorrow. That night while Johnny and I crawl into bunks upstairs from the locker room, I feel that things may not be so bad after all.

Vince, I get to see the next day, is like no one I have ever met before. His skin is a very dark brown. His hair which is kind of long, is slicked down towards the back of his head in real shiny curls like he uses a lot of Vaseline. His face is very thin with teeth that aren't straight. If he were from St. Paul, they would have made him wear braces to fix that.

He does seem pretty angry. Maybe he doesn't like working here: doing the laundry, and mowing the lawn, and fixing things. A few times during the trip he says, "Part of every race known to man is in my blood."

Johnny and I nod. By this time all three of us are bouncing along in Vince's old car. I thought Vince was mean at first, but he just seems mad at something. He's pretty friendly with Johnny and me and drives us to a town called Trenton. He even bought us each a candy bar on the way back. He says he was an orphan. I suppose things can be pretty bad for an orphan, maybe be even harder than being a spy. Vince spent most of the trip just being very quiet looking at the road. I was pretty quiet too, but Johnny, he had a good old time. Noticing things and asking questions. I wonder how someone gets that way.

By Sunday when the other boys started coming, I was glad I know so much about Mary Valley already. The freshman would sometimes ask Johnny and me where things are. Johnny has this way of being friendly towards everybody, like he just knows that they will like him too. All the other boys call him Johnny Jo. They call me Francis.

The next days get all mixed together for me, so many new boys and priests. About one hundred boys, some of them almost men, have come from all over the country to be here. The younger boys like me live in a brick building attached to the big old wood building I saw when I got off the train. We are the high school students. On the first floor of that building is a big room that is our study hall. The second floor is the locker room and in one corner of it is a place for the seniors to sleep. This is a privilege for them. All the rest of us, about sixty kids sleep in two dormitories on the third floor. There is one separate room on the third floor. That is where a priest called the Prefect of Discipline lives. His name is Father Delvechia. He is very short and wears a cassock. He always looks like he needs a shave. He has a small round stomach that sticks out. Very silently he walks through the study hall and locker rooms and dormitories looking at us to make sure we are silent. We need to be silent most of the time here.

No one tells Fr. Delvechia that we can tell when he is coming because he smells like pipe tobacco. It's scary and a little funny to see boys whispering to each other, and then you can tell that they smell him coming and suddenly are very quiet. He still catches boys sometimes, though. They get scolded and sometimes worse. He's not as bad as he sounds.

He's got a sad face. Sometimes I think he smokes so much so we can tell he's coming. In this way he gives us a little chance.

The older seminarians in the final two years of seminary live in the wooden building with the priests. Those guys sleep two to a room and they don't have Fr. Delvechia walking around watching them as much. They live on the first floor. The priests live up on the second floor. The second floor is off limits to seminarians unless you're told to go up and see a priest. This is usually bad news. There is a third floor two, but nobody goes up there. This whole place used to be a resort when Philadelphia was farther away. The way this building is right now you can hardly tell that a long time ago, people used to come here to have fun.

Like an afterthought Vince has a tiny room that opens out of the basement. I don't seem much of him anymore. Occasionally when all of us seminarians are marching through the main wooden building, we see him staring at us from the shadows. I can't tell what he is thinking, but he has this strange deep look in his eyes.

There are two smaller buildings too. One is connected from behind to the big building. It's the chapel. We spend a lot of time there. Underneath the chapel is the refectory. The other smaller building is connected to the dormitory building. Upstairs in this building are the classrooms. A gym is on the first floor. The gym has a smell like the one at my grade school, that funny smell of sweaty boys.

But back to the main building, the old resort, as you enter the main double doors, a grand wooden stairway stands in the middle of the room twisting up to the second floor. Along the walls going up the stairs is dark wood with some designs carved on it. On a landing midway up the stairs is a life size white statue of the Blessed Virgin Mary with a buzzing blue florescent halo. Those calm eyes stare out of the humming blue glow whenever I pass. She seems so peaceful up there holding her rosary and watching over us while she hums.

It was really strange when the first bell rang; all the older guys became absolutely silent and still. Then they commenced like a bunch of ants to march into chapel. I figured out almost immediately that I should just follow. Now I'm used to it. The bell rings sometimes every few minutes, and we then file quietly into chapel, study hall, locker rooms, or class rooms. A couple of times it even rings for recreation, although after doing everything by the bell it's hard to figure out what to do during time that's supposed to be free.

In some ways I like it here. The bell always ring on time, I always know where to go, and I'm never alone except when the bell rings for us to take showers after recreation. Even then we can only stay in the shower for a couple of minutes because there's always a line of boys waiting.

Maybe it's the trip, but I'm more complicated that before. There's the me that's from back home that I remember and the me that's here. As if that isn't enough there's that spy voice that comes from the inside. It notices which boys are handsome and which boys are mean. In some funny way though it doesn't matter who I am, because it's the bell that tell me what to do. The only thing I have to worry about is doing things right. Since we do things over and over again, that's not much of a problem.

I do have a crush on a sophomore. He is tall and athletic. I especially notice that a lot of the other boys like talking to him. I sleep on the bunk above him. When the first bell of the day rings at 6AM and we all jump out of our bunks reciting the Ave Maria in rapid fire, I hardly even get a chance to see him as we file silently down to the locker room. After all we seminarians are almost always moving in silent streams.

Things settle in pretty fast at the seminary because there is no confusion. Four days after we all arrive there is a big party in the evening. In late afternoon of that day we all go up to a field behind the chapel. There's even a little woods back there. The older guys build a big bonfire as night starts edging in. The priests are there too and stand stiffly around the outskirts of the fire with plaid shirts on instead of black cassocks. With awkward respect one or two of the braver seminarians actually go up to talk with them. As the blaze gets bigger and not a single bell rings, the darkness gives each of us enough separateness to remember our homes. A crackling light of memory glows on our faces. We laugh not just in a tight way, but deeply like something running through us.

Then each class puts on a skit. Sometimes it's just telling a joke. Sometimes even funnier, skits poke fun at the priests. Maybe it's the darkness that allows us to do this one time a year. The priests smile awkwardly like they'd really like to be part of the fun if they could.

My class is supposed to put on a skit, but we don't know each other. Finally this guy just rises to the surface and takes charge. He is a strong, handsome, blond guy who looks almost beautiful; the kind of beautiful that is in motion and doesn't care how it looks. He starts telling us what to do; it barely makes sense to me, but I'm included among the select players. What a relief! It's so dark now it hardly matters what happens. Everybody is just waiting for an opportunity to laugh.

Finally Vince who's wearing real tight pants plays an electric guitar and sings "Love Me Tender Love Me True" like he really means it. When he's done with that he turns up his amplifier and plays ferocious rock and roll music. He smiles in a hard way at the priests. We start clapping and cheering. The priests begin to look very uncomfortable. We take the cue and become silent; now it's like Vince doesn't exist any more. We head back to the seminary.

9PM the bells start ringing again; quiet falls over everyone. By next morning when we jump out of bed to recite our Ave Maria's the bonfire seems like a dream.

Over the next couple of weeks there's a funny change. I notice that sophomore I had a crush on has an embarrassed look on his face just like my father. That's when the change starts. First I notice that I don't jump out of my skin every time he walks by. Then I notice that each time I see him he looks a little more lonely and awkward. Finally I just forget to be aware of him when he's around. For the first time in my life I learn that feelings change almost like the weather. When he leaves the seminary a few months after this, I hardly notice.

Time is different in the seminary than in the outside world. Here it is always constant and predictable like the bells. I know exactly what I'll be doing at any time of the day or week. Everything is all figured out carefully. I never have to choose except maybe a little bit for recreation. The regimen may sound very strict, but it lets that voice inside that figures things out, grow by it self. I can just listen and not do anything about it.

Sometimes I do wonder about this a little. As I move along with the bells, I feel like I am eves dropping on the hidden inside voice that notices and figures things out. Sometimes I am not sure which voice is me. It hardly seems like an urgent question because life just keeps going on here.

I find it very easy to be a good boy. All I have to do is to follow the rules. When I see classmates having a hard time I wonder why they just don't follow the rules like me. That's what the priests and God want. There's no need for hidden voices to disturb me being good.

Not that it's always easy being here. Things happen sometimes. Seven boys in my class have decided that they're better than the rest of us. The hang around with each other and call themselves "The Magnificent Seven." For some reason they're mean, glancing at each other a lot and making fun of other kids. Even that blond guy who took charge of the skit slipped in with them. They caught a freshman named Tim Hurley when he was alone during recreation and broke duck eggs from the pond over his head. I thought of my brother Chris and try real hard not to look too lonesome or vulnerable. It helps to have a group of boys to disappear into so you can't be picked out individually. I connect up with boys who get good grades: Johnny, another smart guy named Bob Greco. We aren't up to the standards of "The Magnificent Seven," but they are a little in awe of us because of our grades. Almost all the seminarians settle into little groups, not families exactly because we don't really take care of each other. The seminary comes first. We march in disciplined files or roam in protective clusters.

Besides being in groups there's another kind of way seminarians are together. Some older guys who are louder and more sure of themselves kind of adopt younger boys. These boys are usually short and cute like Johnny. I know that I am too much of a sissy for that to happen to me. It always looks so safe when one of the older guys walks around the pond with a younger boy. But at least I'm part of a group. Terrible thinks can happen to people when they are alone.

Johnny and I are often together. One day during the half hour recreation between lunch and class he asks me kind of formally if I would go for a walk around the pond with him. When we are half way around he stops for a minute and looks at me straight on, the way he usually does, and explains carefully, "You might notice Francis that I'm always turning my head to look at people." He looks at me steadily and straight on as if this were a vital piece of information.

I nod. "Now that you mention it Johnny, I do."

With a satisfied look on his face he goes on. "It's not that I try to do that, but my eyes don't move in their sockets. I've been like this since birth. My mom and dad tried all sorts of doctors but nothing helped. So this is the way I am." His whole head looks down for a moment. Finally he fixes his gaze on me more intently than he usually does like this is some sort of a test, except I'm not sure if the test is for him or me.

I do know that something important is happening so I think a little before saying anything. Just before I fall too deeply into thought, I stop myself short. I know I need to say something pretty quickly so he doesn't think that he seems strange to me. Even though I don't like to look at people straight on, I make an exception with Johnny. I get a little formal too, so he knows I recognize the importance of what he's said. "Thank you for telling me Johnny. I think you're just fine." Then I nod at him and start walking because I don't want to make too big a deal out of this either.

Johnny laughs like something fun has happened. "You're a good old boy, Francis." We finish walking around the pond. The ducks are squawking and we talk about whatever goes through our minds. Later in Latin class I think about Johnny and wonder if it's because of his eyes, that he meets people and things head on. He's too busy directly facing what's happening to glance around and make fun of people or even be scared.

Johnny being around makes playing sports a little more comfortable for me, although he's usually chosen for a team way before I am. Playing sports helps me fit in, so it's pretty important. I try to be even more invisible when The Magnificent Seven start talking about queers. Though unlike at a regular high school back home you can only go so far being mean here, especially about the queer stuff. I've got a hunch about half the boys here are just like me. Of course we don't really talk about it.

Still, the really popular guys, the ones that boys want to be with, are the guys who seem more male and normal, like they might actually have a life if they left here.

At any rate playing sports is where I meet Bernie for the first time. He's a guy that almost everyone wants to be with. It's only about a month or so into the year. When the bell rings this afternoon I head out for the playing fields. Two older guys choose up sides for football. Bernie is one of the older guys, and he has his shirt off. Because it would be a mortal sin, I can't look impurely at men, I have some difficulty looking at him at all. He talks very loud, or maybe it's just everybody gets quiet when he talks.

He disturbs me; with sideways glances I start putting a picture together--wiry, sandy colored crew cut, and coarse stubble poking through his face, wiry hair all over his chest, and he's sweating. That spy voice inside say, "He looks like a bristly pig!" I notice his glasses and the way he has of staring people down and then smiling. He chooses me last; he doesn't know my name and just points at me. I'm stuck in the line rushing and blocking for the next hour and a half. Bernie meanwhile is calling the shots. He has a funny way of touching his bare chest and looking up out beyond the playing field, almost like he's searching for something. Then he flashes back humorously but just a little sad. People do what he says. As I leave the field still hearing his voice, I'm aware of a smell, but not exactly. I don't actually smell anything, but Bernie fills the air.

Chapter 6

In the seminary, time runs so smoothly, it barely seems to pass. I live in a world that seems like forever, only occasionally and reluctantly am I disturbed by my inner voice. I pass Bernie in the halls sometimes. Not a big deal. I do notice though how he sits on the railing of the porch in the evening, his classmates circling. I notice the way he laughs, as if fear and correctness don't exist.

We have assemblies every Friday afternoon; announcements are made; kids are reprimanded for infractions of the rule. Fr. Mark Roberts, the superior of this whole place runs the meetings. He starts with a short sermon on things like faith, obedience or the necessity of showering frequently. He has a reputation for being brilliant, but mostly he looks old. I suppose that might be because his head is bald and his body is shapeless under his black cassock. Still, he radiates power. He speaks with a deep melodious voice while looking at you with eyes that penetrate your scariest secret. He's like my idea of God: deep, mysterious, powerful, and easily angered. During one of these meetings in October right before his sermon he announces, "I have some unfortunate news. Bernard McQuade has the mumps. This can be very dangerous for an adult. A doctor has been in to see him and has ordered that he remain in isolation for a week."

I should have noticed the low rumbling sound, but I suppose it wouldn't have mattered anyway. Out of some little gap in my routine a geyser rushes through shooting me miles above anywhere I have ever been before, and I'm scrambling while being thrust higher and higher out of the confines of my world. My head spins while my stomach bounces up and down. My inner voice whispers with a chuckle, "You're in love with Bernie McQuade. You won't survive if you don't get to see him around." It's only then I notice I've stopped breathing. Gasping for air as quietly as possible I sit up straight and pretend to listen to Fr. Robert's voice, hoping I look inconspicuous…except there's this stabbing yearning inside that I can't begin to touch. How can I get through a week knowing I won't see Bernie? This wasn't supposed to happen with a guy who's loud and bristly like a pig. The careful procession of my life veers off course; the only measure now is my distance from Bernie.

During my most orderly moments, that inner voice frantically whispers, "Where's Bernie?"

I'm not sure when I first started hearing that voice, probably about three because it was after the infection on my penis and before Bud. My family and my dad's two brothers' families all went to Silver Lake that day. My skin felt sunny and warm; I walked a little away from everybody to be closer to the lake. While the sun was shining in a million lights off the wavy lake, I saw this being with jewels dripping down its sides jump out of the water. For one brilliant splashing moment radiance shone in the world and my life. Then I realized that it was a fish leaping in the sun. I almost told everybody about this amazement, but that little voice said, "Don't, they'll never believe you."

I was really lucky that I got some practice with that voice because later that afternoon I really needed it. You see not too long after that, my father and his two brothers, all smooth, brown and bare-chested, decided that each of the three big brothers would carry one of us three little brothers running through the water. I was excited like Christmas morning because the brother with the shiniest, biggest chest picked me. I forget what happened after that; but the next thing I remember I was sitting by the leg of a picnic table, my back turned away from the adults who were all clustered together. They didn't think that I could hear their whispering voices, "Ssshhh! He didn't know what he was doing. ssshhh!" All the while I was staring at paint flaking off the gray wood of that picnic table leg. That was when I heard the inner voice again but more urgently than before, "Francis, be very careful. You mustn't let people know the things you see and the things you want to do. Don't tell anybody, it's our secret."

Chris used to hear a strange voice too but sometimes from the outside. I am very relieved that I don't, because things would be even more complicated if I didn't know from where my voice was going to start popping up from.

It's not so much that the voice bothers me, although it did kind of trick me with Bernie. It mostly just surprises me like having a secret friend who's a little smarter, not so afraid and much more reckless. Whatever that voice is, it hardly seems to care about embarrassment, except when it gets caught. It talks a lot about Bernie now.

Besides becoming more familiar with that inner voice I also start getting pretty good at ping pong, of course that's not really a sport. There is a table in the basement of the dormitory building. Every evening for about forty five minutes we have free time. This is the freest time of the day. There's not enough time to change clothes and play real sports. We can even watch television. Sometimes we walk around the pond mostly in three's or four's. The priest's discourage us from walking in two's, especially if it's with the same person a lot.

Bob Brewer and Joe Hart walked around the pond alone too many times. Bob was in my class, masculine, quiet and sort of lost looking. Joe was one year older, kind of feminine, but real sure of himself. Somehow we all knew that they were told by the faculty not to be alone with each other. Bob and Joe still got together and most us got real quiet and uncomfortable when they came around. We all knew it was just a matter of time until something terrible would happen to them and we didn't want to be too close. Some of the guys in The Magnificent Seven told mean stories about them and took every opportunity to make fun of them. Most guys didn't go that far. I think Bob and Joe were in love with each other.

Then one day their beds were stripped. They disappeared. Actually a couple of the older seminarians saw them being driven away by the prefect of discipline, Fr. Delvechia. He's the one who walks around smelling like tobacco and watches to see that we follow all the rules. When people leave in the way Joe and Bob did it seems like they die; we all huddle together more closely and whisper.

Discipline here is handled in a very comprehensive way here; it touches every part of our lives. Back home I was afraid of many things, but they were so vague; most of the time they didn't even have names. In some ways the discipline here puts a name on my fear--disobedience. Because it is so definite now, life is much easier to handle. There is a simple solution to fear: obedience. Any one who stays here is gradually channeled into maintaining this protection from fear.

At the very top of this disciplining system stands God. Like I said before, He judges pretty severely. After all once you're sent to hell you're a goner. Knowing this helps us stay obedient. Only a few steps down from God is Fr. Roberts, the superior here. I was told that he almost got kicked out when he was a seminarian. This is hard to believe because he is so strict. In spite of his brilliance he must have a pretty bad memory because he always seems so shocked and outraged when seminarians make mistakes. Then there's the prefect of discipline, Fr. Delvechia who lives in the same building as we younger seminarians. He is softer that Fr. Roberts and looks a little sad when he disciplines someone, like he would really rather be doing something other than roaming the halls spying on boys. The rest of the priests are also supposed to maintain the watch too, but sometimes you can tell that they look the other way.

Those are the top levels. The bottom level is made up of us seminarians. The priests choose a school prefect from the seminarians. This seminarian is from the senior class. This important position is given to the most successfully obedient guy. He enforces rules throughout the whole school. This is a very privileged position. Under him are lesser prefects who watch over dormitories, study halls, refectory tables, and work crews. Each class also has a prefect. All prefects have the important responsibility of being a spy for the priests and God.

When someone is reported, if what he did is serious enough, he gets a "D" in discipline. If what he did is really bad, He gets an "F." Fr. Roberts announces these disciplinary grades during the Friday meetings. If a person gets more than one "D" or just one "F," very likely the rest of us will soon find his bed stripped. This is a strong incentive for obedience and most of us do our utmost not to get reported. You have to do your utmost to stay here. I'm not complaining because I have always tried to keep on my toes.

We have to be vigilant at all times because any event can explode into punishment. Twice a year we get to go into Philadelphia for the day just to have fun, but we have to be back absolutely no later than 9PM. Last week when we had this day in Philadelphia a group of four boys were late. We all know that there is never an excuse for being late.

When the 9PM bell rang letting us know that it was time to brush our teeth, get in our pajamas, and crawl into our bunks; we all knew that the guys were missing. It was scary but still exciting like a horror movie wondering what's going to happen to them. We can't talk at nights here, but we all just looked at each other in a very knowing sort of way.

As usual the lights went out in the dormitory at 9:30. Suddenly the light out in the hall way flash on. I can see Fr. Delvechia leading those four guys into the hallway. With a silent sharp chop of his arm he motions them to kneel down on the hallway floor. They are kneeling there so long that I finally fell asleep.

Next morning Fr. Delvechia who usually isn't so severe, interrupts study hall and announces, "There was a very serious infraction of the rule last night. A group of seminarians came back one half hour late. They were given a penance last night, and Fr. Roberts will give them "D's" this Friday. This must not happen again!" He gave a sharp jabbing motion for the benefit of the rest of us, because the four guys who were late had their heads bent over their desks. What scared me most was that those guys weren't trying to make a mistake. Bob Greco who is in my class was one of the late guys. He said the bus they were taking to the train was delayed that night. Bob had always been quiet and ruffled looking, but after this event he started whispering instead of talking. He stopped combing his hair too.

So terrible things happen here too, but they haven't happened to me. I just need to keep trying harder and harder to be perfect. Life on the outside is even more unpredictable. Besides this is becoming my life. Since I have my secret about being homosexual, I have to be especially careful. I have to hide that part of me that is so bad. If I'm not very careful, I can almost see myself, queer and lonely in that world where ex-seminarians go. So to the priests, I'm good. To the other seminarians, I'm nice--maybe a little ordinary. Ordinary sounds pretty good to me. Except for when my inside voice talks about things.

I suppose that's why I like Johnny and I am in love with Bernie. In love...What did I say? They are both part of my ordinary life here, but neither of them seems ordinary. They don't act like they are afraid, and when I am around them I'm not just ordinary. I know that there is a world outside of my fear even if I can't see it.

By the way I'm making a little headway with

Bernie. This happened in the refectory. Part of the responsibility of freshmen is to periodically bus dishes back to the kitchen. Every few weeks I have to put an apron on and all by my clumsy self, go from table to table with a cart picking up dirty dishes. Given my scrambling nervousness, this is an ordeal. Steel willed I set out to do this task as inconspicuously as possible. With tunnel vision I can accomplish this until I get to Bernie's table. No matter how much I narrow my world I'm still aware that I'm in his field of vision. I'm so nervous I keep trying to stick my thumbs into my pockets like an ostrich sticks its head in the sand. Unfortunately my apron covers my pockets. My thumbs with great determination found their havens and pierced through the apron on both sides of my pants. Bernie, who's very alert, notices this. Head down, thumbs safely hidden, I hear his voice say, "Francis." The surprise of his voice saying my name throws me for a loop. Then just in case I thought it was some sort of an accident I hear it again, "Francis, is that a new style of apron?"

The funny thing is that I don't hear the other guys at his table laughing. He's talking soft and private to me, not to score points. I take a quick look up, just enough to see he's smiling looking straight at me like he's saying hello.

Finally things make sense enough so that I can squeeze out a few words to Bernie. "UM, no, my thumbs just slide in there...I'm nervous."

He acknowledges me with a nod and turns back to his audience.

I'm paralyzed with amazement. Bernie who is so wonderful said my name and nodded at me. I exist somewhere in his world. I want to run away before he finds out I don't deserve it, but I want to stay near him, more than anything I know.

Bernie glances back at me. "Well kid, I'll see you around."

"…Ya, Bernie." I actually say his name while taking one last quick look. He's already talking to the other guys like none of this ever happened; except I know it did.

Not everyone is so kind though. Some guys stick meanness behind their humor. This can happen anywhere too. At meals we are assigned to sit with the same five people for three months at a time. A fourth year student sits as the prefect. Then there's a junior, a sophomore, and two freshmen. Edward Perchow is the prefect of my table. I don't know why people make fun of him. He looks tall and strong and has olive skin and a deep voice. I remember seeing him in the bathroom. He was standing at the urinal before stepping into the shower, standing there squarely, towel draped over his shoulder instead of protecting his back side, real nonchalant and natural about his strong body.

He doesn't act like part of the herd, but he doesn't have Bernie's devil may care confidence; even worse, Edward doesn't play sports. He is just separate.

The junior at my table who is always trying to score points with other guys constantly ridicules Edward about how he looks, how eats, and what he says. This junior leads two guys from the table in ridiculing attacks on Edward. I try to look inconspicuous. I understand about being afraid but not about meanness. Mostly I don't want those guys to turn in my direction. I don't like what they do to Edward, but when they focus on him, they can't focus on me. One day wanting to feel more safe, I say something sarcastic to Edward too.

This is the last straw for Edward. He became very still and directs his voice to the junior. "You're just a cowardly bully leading this pack; you ought to be ashamed of yourself." Then he turns to the other two guys. "You guys have a mean streak and are stupid for being led around like this." Then he looks at me in a steady appraising way. "Francis when are you going to grow up and get some backbone?"

Everybody at the table is so silent that I can hear Edward's heavy breaths. Unfortunately by the end of the meal the other guys are back to their normal meanness. My shoulders feel all weighed down by my own meanness. My inside voice says, "This is how it happens. First you're afraid and then you're mean." I hear the voice and kind of understand, but I know the afraid part is something that is just there. It's like breathing. I decide to try to keep quiet when I am afraid.

I remember Rickie Favor from the old

neighborhood in St. Paul. Rickie liked to catch young pheasants when they were still too young to fly. Then he'd hold on to the pheasant's two legs, one in each hand. While the bird screamed, he'd tear those legs apart. All this time he'd be laughing like he enjoyed watching the bird's agony.

Those guys really seem to enjoy tormenting Edward, laughing when they tear him apart. For me, I was afraid and I joined in to feel safer. I don't mean that as an excuse or anything, but that's just how things are.

What if those guys even Rickie, were even more afraid than I am, but they just didn't know it? They may have thought that they were having a good time, but they were really scared to death and just trying to feel safer. I don't know.

This is interesting to me but not a solution for Edward.

Chapter 7

The trip back to St. Paul for Christmas vacation is considerably easier than that first trip. I'm not nearly as afraid because I know dad will pick me up at the bus station and then I can just slide back into a life that provides temporary comfort. It's still a real long trip; I start on Friday evening catching the bus to Philadelphia, and I get into St. Paul 6PM Saturday evening.

I wanted to see my family again so badly when I left, even Dick. I missed them so much I couldn't even thing about it. But then things picked up at the seminary and now I'm not sure if I'm heading home or away from it.

Maybe it's because I'm so tired from being on the bus for so long or that things were pretty bad at home in spite of Saturday nights; but I feel real hazy about returning, like I should feel more excited than I actually do. I try to picture everybody, presents, and lots of food...that helps, especially as the bus hits the outskirts of St. Paul.

Spot lit Christmas trees in picture windows make the dark yards piled up with snow look friendly. I especially like flocked Christmas trees with ornaments all the same shape and color. The pastel puffy regularity of those trees makes me think that the family in there really knows how to live right, the kind of family that has professional pictures taken of them every year where everybody is smiling. My family uses all kinds of different Christmas ornaments. All the tinsel doesn't hide the fact that there is just a regular green tree underneath. We never have professional pictures taken either. In our pictures there is always a person missing who is taking the picture. That missing person is usually my dad.

Dad is waiting for me. When he sees me step off the bus he looks relieved that I made it and that he got the time of the arrival right. We both then stare at each other for a minute, not quite believing that this is the correct person after all. Like it takes a minute for us to gloss over the discrepancies in our memories.

"Hi son."

"Hi dad, good to see you. It sure was a long trip." I grab the suitcase that the bus driver has already unloaded. I pick it up and start walking even though I don't know where the car is.

"Francis let me take it; you've had a long trip." He seems like he's kind of afraid of me, and I'm all tight and not sure I can let anybody take care of me. He catches up to me, puts his arm around me, and I just let the suite case go.

"Sure dad." I think we finally recognize each other. We don't say much in the car, but we never have, so things are back to normal.

When we get home and I step into the door, my mother is running the kitchen sending my brothers on various missions.

"Chris will you set the table? Dick why don't you go out to the freezer and get those frozen pie crusts?"

Immediately I recognize the order and feel at home. Mom and I hug casually. I take over the second lieutenant position. No words spoken; we just recognize what we need to do.

Besides fitting back in to the order of the house, the next most important thing I do is become a celebrity. My family brings me on formal visits to grandmothers and other relatives. My cousins, who have become normal teenagers, can't quite make sense of me; I like that confusion; it feels safer.

I don't have much time for Chris during those days, and at night he just roles over right to sleep like he's real tired. Dick is too squirrelly to talk much even if there were time. He's got to make everything go faster than it already is, and I just want a more regular speed.

What with all the activity and the way I know I don't really belong, the vacation goes by in a heartbeat. I think I'm caught in a misunderstanding, being from a place where I am becoming a different person from what people remember. Of course no one else knows this.

The last night Chris is silent, but he's moving

around a lot as if to signal that he's not asleep. I am trying half heartedly to sink my heels in and stop the sliding into tomorrow. He must have heard me.

"Francis are you all right?"

"Sure Chris, sometimes it's a little hard to be always going places."

"You know, you can stay at home if you want to."

I lie there very still, thinking. I have heard while I've been home that Chris is getting beaten up in high school, and I remember those comic books. I turn around to face him studying him like I'm saying good bye, "I'm fine Chris, I want to go back; I really do."

I know Chris can't say that he wants me to stay because I'd just say no and something would be torn from him again that can't be put back.

"Well Francis, you take care of yourself." Chris sounds like he really means it and in some way understands.

He looks like he's sleeping when I leave the next morning. Mom says goodbye in the kitchen; she's getting ready to do laundry. We both have things to do today. Once again I become my dad's quiet guest. Once again he silently watches me sitting in the bus as it roles out of his world.

I see Christmas decorations stubbornly shining in the dark streets of Chicago on this January third. Something breaks my heart about it, not just that this Christmas is over, but that Christmases always end before you can feel them. If only people would take those decorations down right away.

Chapter 8

Mostly, when I get back, bells, silence, studying, uncomfortable sports--I feel, it's my place. I'm sitting with a new group of guys in the refectory; they're pretty friendly. Johnny is one of them. All of us joke around, and it feels safe. In some ways it's better than a family because you know it's not forever.

I make the mistake of letting Fr. Delvechia, who not only is prefect of discipline but also runs the choir, know that I used to play the piano. When I was in the seventh and eighth grades I would walk about a mile to visit Pearl, the piano teacher.

She lived alone in a little trailer surrounded by woods at the end of a steep ravine. She had many, many cats and when I would open the door there was a piercing, sour smell. She'd always be sitting very dramatically at the piano dressed like a gypsy. She used a lot of red color on her cheeks. Then she would jump up from the bench as if my arrival were an amazing and longed for occurrence. It was the first time I saw someone wear bracelets.

I never practiced much, but I played the first half of the Moonlight Sonata over and over again real slow using the loud pedal. She thought I was a genius and bought me a gold piano pin to wear. Periodically at the end of the lesson she would call to the back of the trailer and a different man, each time, would come out. Usually he looked a little younger than her and had flushed skin. He'd look strong in a worn out sort of way. I always felt a little sick to my stomach as she proudly asked me to shake his hand. I didn't want to think about why he was there in the morning. In some fairy tale way I was frightened of becoming like her.

Unfortunately Fr. Delvechia doesn't know that I only play the Moon Light Sonata, and then only the first part. When the regular organist is away on a trip, Fr. Delvechia tells me that I'm supposed to play the organ for Sunday Mass. I spend most of Saturday trying to learn the hymns, but I have a strong feeling that this is not going to work. Sunday morning comes. During Mass my fingers stumble across the keys making a wild racket. Most of the hymns aren't recognizable. As the seminarians leave chapel I see some of them, especially The Magnificent Seven laughing as they look toward the organ behind which I'm peeking. To me it feels like I want to just crawl under the organ and not wake up.

I know the chapel isn't empty yet because I still smell the sweet sour smokiness of Fr. Delvechia. I want to slip away, but I know he's still around. Finally I hear the soft tread of his feet. The steps come up to the organ and stop. I know that I need to do something, so I stick my head up over the top of the organ getting ready to be shot.

I see Fr. Delvechia's face peering over the organ looking for me. He doesn't look mad. He just says, "Well there you are Francis."

The chapel is dark now. His short pot bellied silhouette stands in front of me. He looks like he is thinking about something.

I look down to the ground. "Hi Father...I'm really sorry it didn't turn out so well." I don't say anything more because I'm in this deep hole of embarrassment and even looking up makes it feel deeper. I can just barely make out that he's taking out his pipe and stuffing it with that tobacco of his. It helps me to think that he's not just staring at me. I peek up again. He's bending toward me a little; I can make out his face; it's soft like punishment would be the last thing he is thinking of. He smiles faintly at me.

I look away again.

He clears his throat.

I take this a signal and look up.

He catches my glance and smiles almost mischievously. "Well some of those songs got a little rough, but there were no fatalities and we all got through unharmed--so you need a little practice." He shrugs his shoulders then actually lights his pipe in chapel and smiles at me like we share a little secret. I know he's not going to punish me now. I don't really understand why. It seems like part of him wants to comfort people no matter how bad they mess up, and part of him makes people kneel outside his door for hours. I wonder if it's confusing for him too.

We leave the chapel together silently. I join a line of guys going to the refectory. Someone makes a funny remark about the hymns and then people just forget. I then understand that if you play your cards right and are not to conspicuous, everybody else is too involved with their own problems to remember anything for too long.

Generally I have reputation for being a pretty embarrassed guy. There is something innocent about looking embarrassed that stops a lot of guys from joking at me too hard. I guess I'm not much of a challenge.

I start extending my circle a little, beyond Johnny, Bob Greco to another guy named Tim Hurley. I know how important it is to do that especially in the seminary where people all of a sudden disappear. I also start talking with someone new in my class, Gene Ryan. He is pretty friendly with The Magnificent Seven, but is kind of like a mascot. He's short and round but has a big joking voice. He laughs in a loud way that lets you know that you're in on something real funny that other people may not be smart enough to understand.

There's something real fluttery about him when he gets around athletic guys, but then he laughs real loud and everybody wants to be in on the joke. He likes to point out two worn-through holes on the inside of his pants by the crotch right below his zipper, and says, "My balls have teeth! ha! ha! ha!"

The first time I heard it, I thought it was pretty funny, but I really didn't want to imagine it much.

Gene and I now go on walks a couple of times a week. He never plays sports and gives me an excuse to stay off the playing field once and a while. I keep the number of our walks to a couple of times a week because of how the priests discourage walking with the same person too much. You can never be too careful.

Sometimes I don't always want to know what Gene has on his mind. In Latin class we were studying Julius Caesar and the priest off handedly mentioned Cleopatra. We giggled. After class Gene asks me to go for a walk as if something important has happened. We start walking around the pond that was almost thawed but still grey and spongy.

"Hey Francis, how did you like Latin class today?" He laughs like we're both in on a joke.

"All right, it's funny how words are placed in a different order than in English. It can be pretty confusing."

"I bet Cleopatra got it whenever she wanted it." He commences to push his round hips forward in a jerking motion and laughs even louder.

"I suppose so." I feel all tight.

"She really had the pick of the guys any time she felt like it! ha! ha! ha!"

We were walking side by side and he stops to look at me real intently, like he's searching for some particular response, sort of in code. But I feel this funny danger, like if I don't do this right Gene might be angry. Between the memory of what he said about his balls and the scary way he moves his hips, I just condense to some corner of my body and smile at him a little embarrassed, like maybe after all I really am not in on the joke.

He finally snaps, "Never mind," and laughs maybe even at me.

We finish walking around the pond like nothing has happened and are still pretty friendly, but I think we're both a little more careful with each other.

A few days after this the pond completely clears of ice. While Johnny and I are walking around it I look up on the hill and for the first time in my life I see dogwoods blooming, big impossibly floppy white butterfly petals settling on bare branches. For a moment I'm surprised like something is opening up in me, there's something alive and surprising inside me that can come out. I like spring; it makes things seem possible. And sure enough pretty soon the tulip trees bloom, and then the apple trees, and then it's a summer day. Bernie has started to say hello to me once and a while.

Everybody seems happier this last month, like secretly we are congratulating each other for having accomplished something very difficult. There's an exciting question underneath too: who's coming back next year? Parents of some of the boys pick them up on that last day, but most of us take the train and then scatter in all directions.

Chapter 9

First summer home, popping and sizzling bacon in the morning while I'm waking up; smells like heaven. You see food in the seminary is pretty simple. In the morning, there's cold cereal and toast. For lunch, there's a sandwich, usually baloney, plus a bowel of clear soup with a few noodles and grated carrots in it. Canned fruit comes after. For supper, we get something like meatloaf and mashed potatoes, plus a canned vegetable. A piece of cake may follow that. When I left for the seminary I didn't eat vegetables much. I do now. Once and a while guys get food packages from home, these are carefully guarded and shared with only their closest confederates. The smell of bacon in the morning really is a big deal.

I can hear mom setting things in order in the kitchen, getting ready for breakfast. For a few moments I just take it in. Chris is still sleeping or at least lying still in bed. I'm now a guest around here and people are really careful of me. I want to keep on my toes.

In the first week I notice how almost everybody

here is beginning to justify their behavior to me, sharing nervous little confidences. Already the confessional shades my relationships. It's a lonely relief. More and more, people at home don't expect me to be human. My past self flattens into a holy picture, a sacred screen behind which I can think and feel things in secret. And I feel pangs of loneliness for Bernie. I want to hear his name. Once in a while very casually, I mention it, "Ya, there's lots of nice guys in the seminary: Johnny, Tim...oh ya, and Bernie Mcquade."

I'm surprised my family doesn't feel the room shake. I understand now why we bow our heads at the name of Jesus. When I say, "Bernie," even my knees fold. Fortunately nobody notice my knees.

Being with my family feels safer now; I follow their prospects from a distance. It's not exactly that I don't care, but things seem pretty hopeless. I may be like them, but I can get away. The price is that I can't really play with them anymore.

Chris is still being beaten up regularly on the bus trip to high school. He gets up very early to walk to school now. I don't like to imagine how alone he is. His face increasingly freezes into a stare and then something flashes wild in his eyes. Being an outsider, I don't need to think about that as much. My oldest brother Dick is getting by, but he seems lonely too. No one calls him up. He doesn't talk about classes or teachers, as if he's not even going to school.

Maybe as an antidote to all this, my dad has this

big idea. A couple weeks after I get home, he lets us in on his plans while we're all sitting around the dinner table. "Joan, I've got it all set up. I have two weeks off in July, and I want to take you and the kids camping."

"Bill, are you sure we're up to this?"

"Hey kids, what do you think?"

Chris and Dick make a large enough sound for all three of us.

Over the next two weeks my mother begins to plan for every eventuality: boxes of food, pans, plates, little clear bags of plastic utensils, jackets, candles just in case, and prayer books for Mass on Sunday. Chris takes care of the fishing supplies, trying out each rod and reel. Dick goes with dad to pick up a tent at Wards. I'm not so sure about any of this.

The night before the trip the living room is piled high with boxes and bags, stray fishing poles sticking out. Next morning my dad gets up very early and begins packing the car with concentrated purpose. None of us, even Bill stay in bed much past sunrise. After a quick breakfast, we all watch in suspense as dad is trying to figure out how to squeeze those last boxes in the car. His audience hardly rattles his concentration.

Then we're off, considerably later than expected. At noon, to me we don't seem nearly far enough along; we stop anyway and open one of those boxes pulling out sandwiches and cool aid. We sit at the road side stop like a real American family. My dad looks proud.

We start up again. At 4PM, for a real treat, we

eat at an "A&W" Root Beer Stand. We're all getting a little tired, but so far, so good.

We finally get to the state park; dad talks to the ranger and buys a permit like he's done this many times before. When we get to the camp site it's getting pretty shadowy. Dad continues his command and from the back of the station wagon passes boxes out to us.

That's when I notice dad starting to go into slow motion, like something's bothering him that he can't talk about. Dick, ever attentive to any thing out of the ordinary starts in, "Hey dad lets put the tent up."

"Dick, let me take my own time here, you're always going to fast."

"Dad, I don't see those tent poles we bought."

"Joannie, would you stop Dick from bothering me? I need to concentrate!"

Dick has a Geiger counter for finding trouble, but instead of running away, he jumps in the middle of it, "Where are the tent poles dad, huh, dad? I'm only asking a question!"

Somewhere in the ruckus between dad and Dick, we all discover that the tent poles never got to the pile in the living room. Dad keeps saying, "You shouldn't have rushed me," to no one in particular.

Mom is very quiet until dad says, "Joannie, you have got to help me control these kids. I can't do everything!"

This is a cue. "Bill! You forgot the polls."

Then, it's not just Dick and dad, but Dick, dad, and mom going at it. All this time it is getting darker.

Finally dad sneaks into the woods to find branches to prop up the tent from the inside. This probably would have worked, except it starts raining.

Mom and I are the first to crawl into the car about mid way through the night. Dick comes next, pretty wet. Even Chris finally surrenders and joins us. Somewhere around 6AM, my dad gets into the car, not saying much of anything.

By this time a lot of the boxes and bags are wet; by general consensus we decide to go home later that morning to dry out. Everyone is very quiet in the car, even Dick. When we get back mom directs us where to put all the wet things.

The vacation makes the rest of the summer seem pretty easy, but come September, I am ready to go back to the seminary. At home, things just seem to be on the road to somewhere I don't want to go.

Mom and I say goodbye in the kitchen, like we both know what we're doing. Dad uncertainly brings me to the bus station again. For no good reason I cry a little as I board the bus.

When I sit down and the bus starts rolling away, I remember a dream I had when I was very young. I was sitting at the top of stairs leading to the outside. My family was in the basement apartment below me unwrapping Christmas presents. I knew that at any moment someone was going to come by and machine gun them all down. I didn't think to warn them, or maybe I knew it was too late. I just made sure I had an escape route.

Chapter 10

When I get back I find that six guys have quit from my class. We don't spend a lot of time missing people here. The real good news is that a total of four of these guys were from The Magnificent Seven. Even better, the three guys who I hang around with all came back: Johnny, Tim, and Bob. That doesn't even count Gene who I still basically get along with. The important thing is that "we" now out number The Magnificent Seven. The remainder of The Seven now seem more like The Bewildered Three. They wonder around looking lost. They used to focus on some lonely guy and pass around a look between themselves that was both laughing and menacing. As they passed this look back and forth they would build up momentum until one of them would take the lead in playing a dirty trick. They can't pass that look around this year; there's not enough of them.

This year I have become friendly with a classmate from New Jersey called Mario Savio. The guy he hung around with quit over the summer leaving Mario pretty exposed. Mario is short, but too serious and quiet to be adopted by one of the older guys. We go for walks and don't say much to each other, but I think we both know what it is like to be lonely. With The Magnificent Seven disintegrating I feel more open to things.

But the biggest news is that I have decided to try to stop being a spy. Every seminarian has to pick a spiritual advisor. You're supposed to tell him all your secrets. My first advisor mostly told me about his inner ear infections. One of the older guys told me that Fr. Ford reads off a long list of sexual sins and asks you to let him know which ones you do. I decide that Fr. Ford is my man.

He is very short and kind of like a spring all tightly wound up. I can almost hear something inside straining to get out. His coarse orange hair is cut short in a crew cut. That's not the main thing that you notice though; it's the back of his neck. Right above the back of his stiff white clerical collar all sorts of irregular little craters cover the fleshy part of his neck. It makes me think of Swiss cheese. He's got a deep strong voice, but sometimes when he seems relaxed that voice slips into a higher register that's kind of pleading. Once and a while he goes crazy. In class things will be going normally, then all of a sudden the chalk he's using breaks or the ink runs out of his pen. In a flash he starts screaming at us. I'm not too scared of him because those attacks usually don't focus on one person. I even like him because I can see something is eating him up on the inside. If anybody can understand me it'll be him.

After I pick him as spiritual directors, Fr. Ford sends me a note inviting me up to his room on the second floor of the old resort building. Rain drips from the eves of the old porch that evening. Something in me focuses on the dripping sounds so I don't have to think too much about what I plan to do. The lights from town are closed off by the fog. The front porch hangs off the hill like a ship on a quiet sea.

I climb the stairs past the buzzing Madonna, up to the forbidden second floor where priests walk around in plaid shirts. I knock on the door softly and hear a gravelly, deep voice from within, "Come in." Fr. Ford smiles quickly and tensely. "Sit down Francis." Almost right away he explains that he always goes over a list of special problems with new spiritual advisees. "Tell me if you do any of these things." He shoots me a meaningful glance. I nod frightened, but hopeful. He starts reading a list, gradually building momentum, "bestiality, sodomy," and he works his way through a list of names that completely go by me because I don't understand them. I keep looking for a name that I can confess to, but his pace keeps accelerating, "fellatio," I see my opportunity slipping away. Still nothing sounds remotely like anything I feel about Bernie. Finally I can tell he's finishing up. I decide I have to say something or I've lost my chance to really speak with somebody, maybe forever. He finishes his litany with, "necrophilia."

I say, "Yes."

His face that had been resting on one hand, raises up for a quick almost curious look. For a second his face becomes dark with foreboding outrage, but as he looks at me longer his eye brows go up and he only seems troubled. Then he gathers himself by grasping his knees with his hands and looks intently at me. "Francis, do you know what that means?"

"No Father."

"Then why did you say yes?"

"Because it was my last chance. You didn't say the word for what I wanted to talk with you about."

He looks relieved enough to release his grip on his knees and stop looking at me. His face now rests in the palm of his hand like priests do when they hear confessions. "My son, what do you want to tell me?"

This is the moment. Everything freezes. For what seems like forever I listen to those dripping sounds outside and then my hidden self plays a sudden trick on me. It starts running impossibly fast and then with me as a passenger leaps off a cliff beyond my imagination. "I'm attracted to men, Father."

He buries his head deeper into his thick hand and breathes heavily a few times. There's just the suggestion of a little tremor running through his muscular body. He looks at me long enough now to catch my nervousness, caressing it lightly with reassurance. He looks protective and maybe something more that I don't understand. Then there's silence, and

I hear myself inhaling in quick erratic gasps, like after crying.

Finally he says with a strange mixture of gentleness and strictness, "No one can have sex here, Francis. As long as you don't commit that act, it doesn't matter who you are."

It begins dawning on me that I have survived this exposure, not only that, but the world around me has not shattered. He looks at me with a smile as warm and easy as the first day of spring. I almost want to touch his broad face even with that stuff on his neck. The whole room seems to watch us as we see each other in some unexpected way.

Then abruptly it's over. He announces, "You can go now," and releases me from his attention. I want to say all sorts of things to him like how glad I am he listened to me and how much I like him, but he's staring at his desk now; it's time for me to go. Before I turn away I steal one last look at him and catch something plaintive lingering on his face.

Now the foggy night outside the windows seems to veil some miracle just waiting for me. It's now past 9:45 PM and as I walk down the stairs I'm absolutely alone; everyone has been in their beds for fifteen minutes. For once and all alone I fill up that grand staircase and pause just for a moment in the shadowy high ceilinged front room. Then I scurry to the locker room, quickly take my clothes off, and slip into my pajamas. I hear my bare feet padding to the dormitory which is silent except for the sound of creaking bed springs. I want to flash the lights on and yell out to everyone, "I belong here." Instead I crawl into the sheets knowing I'm a person with a real future, me just as I am.

Next morning as usual we are shocked awake by the bell as lights are switched on. As I jump out of bed I feel the icy cold of the floor and drone with all the other sleepy automatic voices, "Ave Maria ..." Then I remember I belong here and smile.

Chapter 11

In our second year, Johnny, Mario, Gene and I start playing a card game called pinochle a couple of times a week. Sometimes we don't even change out of our white shirts and black pants. Bob comes by to watch us play, but he continues to become more silent and almost invisible. He not only doesn't comb his hair now, but he has almost completely stopped changing his clothes. We ask him to play with us sometimes but he just shakes his head like our asking him has disturbed something private going on inside. Tim usually drops in too. Most afternoons he finds out of the way places to study, although he's already real smart. He and Johnny run neck and neck to get the highest grades, although it's mostly Tim racing. He's friendly when he comes around but always looks a little shocked that we aren't studying. He always gets this urgent solemn look on his face whenever he talks about tests; we get lots of tests. When he's not talking about grades or tests he gets kind of limp and seems to not know what to do with his face or hands.

He has solved this dilemma by drilling his right index finger against his right nostril, not exactly inside the nostril but pretty close.

American history book in hand, Tim drops by the card game as if he is the messenger from some more important realm. "Hi guys. Have you all finished studying for the history test? I think I've memorized all the dates." He then scrutinizes us as if he's appraising our chances of passing. Our concentration stays with the card game except for a brief generalized, "Hi Tim." Still determined, Tim pushes ahead. "Johnny what grade did you get in that Latin quiz?"

"I did fairly well, Tim."

Tim pauses as he continues to watch us slap cards down, except with each card he becomes more limp and nervous. He starts smiling and pressing his finger in that drilling motion against his nostril. He finally stops and for a moment looks like he's got urgent business to do even if we don't understand. "I'm going to get ready for that geometry test on Friday. Have you guys started studying yet? It's supposed to be a tough test. Oh by the way, I saw Bernie and some of the seniors fixing that fence by the pond." He disappears somewhere to study. "See you Tim," echoes across the room from the direction of our card game.

The rest of the game feels like being tortured on the rack for me. Other than passing Bernie in the halls, I haven't really seen him this year. This is my chance and I'm missing it. Finally the game ends. While trying to look very calm, I ask Gene if he wants to take a walk around the pond. We still have forty five minutes until study hall. He agrees. I decide not to think about how Gene might figure what I'm doing, since he is an expert on seeing through things like this. We start down to the pond. I hear Bernie's voice not too distant, and since I can't look at him impurely, I direct my gaze to the ground just a couple feet in front of me. As Gene is leading me forward I catch Bernie in my peripheral vision, and my God, his shirt is off, nonchalantly hanging out of his back pocket. His chests shines like it is illuminated from the inside…it glows. The inside voice mutters, "How could you have ever thought he looked like a pig?"

Out of the corner of my spying eye, Bernie looks like that picture of Ulysses that I saw a long time ago, all confident and physical; chest strong and powerful. For a second I feel like that hungry looking Circe. Then I remember that if I really look at his chest I commit a mortal sin. If I confess this to Fr. Ford, he'll know I'm being sexual. Not only will he be angry and disappointed, but I may loose my chance to stay here. Embarrassment, expulsion from the seminary, and eternal punishment stand just in front of me with his shirt off. I recommence looking at the ground.

As Gene is leading me passed Bernie I'm very careful about this test of virtue. With determination worthy of martyred virgins I don't look at Bernie. If I do accidentally slide my vision across his naked chest a few times, the voice inside assures me that it's only to prevent myself from running into a tree. During one of these inadvertent gazes I see Bernie looking at me, puzzled but smiling. Gene and I keep walking until it's all over. I'm none the worse for wear at least in terms of mortal sin. After all mortal sin is a one way ticket hell, and I have things I need to do.

Chapter 12

Towards the middle of the year, we have what's called a retreat to help us keep on our toes. A retreat is a time when classes are called off and for a few days you spend even more time in chapel praying and listening to sermons. In between frequent visits to the chapel there is even stricter silence. Usually a priest from outside the seminary runs the retreat and gives the sermons.

The Friday before the retreat during assembly, Fr. Roberts announces that he chose a priest who has a reputation as a powerful preacher and an expert on adolescents. Fr. Roberts says "adolescents" with a kind of a burning ring in his deep voice. His pink faced shapeless body bends toward us as he starts describing this book called *Catcher in the Rye*. It seems there's this guy named Holden Caulfield who is pretty confused. Father is very relieved that at least we seminarians are sheltered from all this difficulty. For a moment he grows quiet almost like he is loosing himself in that scary story. Then the sharpness flashes back into his eyes and he wishes us all a good retreat. Sunday evening we all file into chapel instead of study hall; this is a dramatic break in our routine. It's a dark night in late November. When we enter chapel I see that the pulpit is spotlighted in the gloom. Outside a storm has been brewing all afternoon, rumbling sounds crash in the distance. We sit silently waiting. Then a priest steps out of the darkness and into the light. His hair is shiny black with gun metal grey strands running through it. He looks polished the way some people do when they know nothing can touch them. His eyes look hard when he smiles.

As he opens up the retreat those rumbling sounds come closer and a howling wind backs up his voice like some spooky organ. He looks out at us for a few minutes, like he is entering inside us and examining every place that we don't want to talk about. Something snaps inside him as he has been electrocuted by some horrible vision. He collects himself and now his voice soothes us like a lullaby, as if only he can protect us from that wild wind that is assaulting the roof with pounding rain. The wind screams, but he keeps comforting us. "Several years ago, there was a very nice boy. His family loved him very much and tried to teach him how to be good." The priest emphasizes the word "good" with restrained ecstasy. Then he pauses smiling again at each of us. "There had been a snow storm just a day before and this nice boy wanted to go sliding in that soft, new snow on the hill above his house. Because he was a nice boy, he asked his mother for permission. His mother who wanted him to help her with chores that day said, "No." Again the priest paused, making sure we were all following that soothing trail of his words. "Now this nice boy decided that he wanted to go sliding anyway. He thought that he had enough time." The priest dragged out the word "time" with relish. "While that boy was sliding he hit a tree and died." The priest's eyebrows now raise and his eyes begin to look glazed. As the wind screeches outside he trumpets at the top of his voice, "That boy went straight to hell! To hell forever!"

Now even the bravest among us, maybe even Bernie, silently shutter as the echoes of this voice join the terrifying wildness outside.

Chapter 13

I keep learning how to be more careful. And then it's Christmas vacation. It's getting clearer to everybody in St. Paul, even Chris that I'm just a guest in that house that I used to live in. Things are really about the same there except more distant to me. Chris and I don't talk much anymore. I suppose it's best this way. Dick looks like he's not going to make it through his first year of college. He's talking about going to officers' training school. Since there's no war going on, this might be a solution for him. Mom and dad are about the same. Just like the bus I keep taking, I'm always in transit, always leaving again. It's easier to forget about things from this vantage point.

Then back I'm back in the seminary again. Things are set up here to help you forget. Even exciting events like vacations and French toast every Friday morning slip and sink into something more important, obedience. Almost everything in the seminary is set up to help us successfully achieve this goal. Choices are trimmed away so smoothly that you hardly remember they were ever there. I have a real talent for giving up choices.

One of my classmates named Joe Walsh leaves at about this time. He isn't part of my circle, but he never belonged to The Magnificent Seven either. He always bounced around between different groups never quite fitting in comfortably anywhere. He had a funny way of looking at you, half joking like nothing matters and half asking for something that he knows he won't get. He hadn't settled in yet to be good or bad, funny or embarrassed, athletic or smart. It's almost like he couldn't take on one of these roles. Maybe he thought he wasn't good enough or that people should like him the way he is. In his last few weeks here guys got uneasy around him. Before he left he came up to me, "Hey Francis what do you say we go for a walk?"

I said, "OK, Joe." He looked even more in between things than usual.

"Francis, no one else knows, but I'm leaving the seminary tomorrow morning. Fr. Delvechia is taking me to the train station."

Even though people here disappear, I've never talked to someone before it happened. I didn't know what to say because inside I'm mostly relieved it's not me. If he's leaving, he must have done something wrong, or maybe he didn't have a vocation to the priesthood in the first place. I covered this thinking up and said as sincerely as I could, "I hope you'll be all right. We'll miss you here."

We kept walking for a while and didn't say much

of anything else. Then he shrugged his shoulders like whatever it was he wanted, he knew he was not going to get. He smiled a little like everything was a joke that only he understands. Next morning his bed was stripped.

Even though I'm still relieved that it's Joe who left and not me, I'm trying harder to do things perfectly. I start taking cold showers on Fridays during lent to commemorate the suffering of Christ. It stops me from thinking about things too much.

When I think of Bernie I inhabit a place far away from stripped beds; he doesn't seem afraid. He's like an ocean of limitless daring. When he smiles, especially when he smiles at me, I'm in this place where nothing else matters except the feeling of his presence lapping all around my shore.

The last couple months of the semester I'm assigned to Bernie's work crew. He's the prefect and there are four of us under him. Six days a week he meets with us and assigns us tasks. Our crew is supposed to keep the gym and the class rooms clean. This means that six days a week I'm actually supposed to be with him. A lot of the time when I report for work he's already there, sitting on the edge of the stage on the north side of the gym, all alone. Bernie doesn't exactly wait; that's for people like me who are either hungry for or afraid of what might happen. Time and space are concentrated around Bernie. He sits on that edge of the stage, an eternal present out of which time issues. Six days a week now I enter into this mystery. He's there gently tapping his worn tennis shoe heels on the edge of the stage, a far off slightly sad look on his face; his taps measuring time for all of us around him.

I can even make a little eye contact with him. I get so close I can see his teeth and hear his breath when he leans toward me to tell me what to do.

Every morning after the wake up bell I'm aware I'll be seeing him soon. It assures me to know that I am following the rules here, I supposed to see him. But my most pressing concern is that he's moving on next year to the second stage of the seminary in Washington DC. This loss hangs over me and I spend much of my time imagining solutions, but it's all just imagining. I get a little distracted; fortunately no one is close enough to me to figure out what is going on. Since I'm not sinning, even my spiritual director Fr. Ford doesn't know about it. Being so easily and successfully good, I have a couple of months without interruption to imagine solutions to the Bernie problem.

Life here rides smoothly until one lunch time Fr. Roberts calls me to the priests' table. It's a real complement that the superior of the whole place wants me to do something for him. "Francis, tell the four juniors washing dishes that assembly will be fifteen minutes early today."

I immediately set out to pass on this important message. I go back to the kitchen and relay it to a junior named Rich. He says that he'll tell the others. I leave thinking how really easy it is to do things right.

The assembly time comes and I notice that these juniors aren't present. So does Fr. Roberts, and taking their absence as willful defiance, he gives each of them a "D" on the spot. For a junior to get a "D" is pretty ominous. After all seminarians should be smoothed out by that time. I have a sinking feeling that there is a problem, and somehow I'm involved.

Sometime during the afternoon another one of the four dish washers, Tom Kelly comes up to me, "Thanks for letting us know about the assembly. You should be the one getting the D. He's angry in a way I have seldom seen someone be, burning cold like dry ice.

Suddenly I realize that Rich didn't pass the message on to his classmates. Tom must think I'm a real rat. As he turns from me sharply like he can barely control himself, I say, "I told Rich, he said that he would tell you guys." Tom still keeps walking. I don't even have time to say, "It's not my fault!"

I immediately go to the rec room to find Rich; I know that he can make everything right again. I find him standing alone like he's waiting for something. I say, "Rich, you remember, I told you about the assembly; didn't you tell the other guys?"

Rich looks pretty genial. Shrugging his shoulders he says, "Don't worry. It'll pass over. Don't bother about it."

"Rich, you gotta tell the guys I told you."

His smile turns hard and he walks away. I know that he will never tell anybody.

I try one last thing; I see Fr. Roberts in the hallway and try to explain what happened. He looks impatient with my long story, especially with the part about not wanting to be blamed. Then I make a major mistake, I say, "They shouldn't get D's, it's not their fault."

Pinning me down with his stare, Fr. Roberts say, "Are you questioning my authority? I said that they have D's. It doesn't matter what happened." For the third and last time this day someone turns their back on me. With Fr. Roberts especially, that's very dangerous. I know that there is nothing more I can do for anybody including myself. Only the bells and the routine can cover things up. After all if there's an accident, somebody's got to pay. It strikes me as strange though how many people are involved in an accident. It's hard to tell where it really starts and stops unless you're the one who pays. Tom Kelly never really talks to me after this but just eyes me suspiciously. Guys here rumor that Rich will be quitting at the end of the year.

Between the seminary routine and Bernie, this accident is fortunately covered up. About a month before the end of the year a guy named Darryl and myself are helping Bernie clean the classrooms. Darryl is in Bernie's class. Darryl smiles softly and keeps out of trouble. I like him; it's like he's been smoothed down by the seminary, but there's still a knowing smile in his eyes like he remembers things. Even though it's clear that we both seek out every opportunity to be with Bernie, Darryl treats me kindly, not competitively.

Being Saturday here, life is a little more relaxed. Out of the clear blue sky Bernie says to Darryl and me, "I bet you two guys couldn't take me on." He growls, "I dare you!"

I can't believe it. His words speed by too fast for me to catch them. Darryl though is not caught unawares; he says without skipping a beat, "Sure Bernie, we'll take you on." I feel this enormous gratitude to Darryl for including me in on something that he and Bernie seem familiar with.

Now normally I'd be terrified to do something like wrestling. You can get a D for that. Almost like I have amnesia, this no longer matters. My inner voice keeps reassuring, "Go on, you can do it, it'll be okay. It's not a sin; it's part of your job"

Darryl and I aren't ferocious fighters. Something about the way we all roll around makes me think that he, like my self is doing something a little more complex than fighting. I do get a chance for one private, close moment with Bernie. He has me in a head lock. I'm struggling just hard enough to force him to hold me tight; for a whole moment my head is pressed against his chest. I see his gray undershirt up close, the weave even. My inner self and outer self are squeezed together and in solitary singleness as I feel the dampness of his body on me right cheek; for a moment I, Francis, hear Bernie's heart beat. And then it's over. Darryl and I don't make eye contact but walk away in silent understanding.

It's only after this brief, wondrous event that a real

course of action dawns on me about Bernie's leaving. Something rises up out of all my imagining. I'll ask him if I can write to him next year.

During the last work period before summer break I bide my time just waiting for the right opportunity. We are both sweeping a classroom floor together. This is it; I know it. My inner self starts running and then leaps off the edge. "Bernie if somebody were to write you at the Washington seminary, would you write back?"

He looks at me like he both understands what I'm really asking but doesn't quite want to answer. Finally he says with a patient and then a relenting, ironic grin, "Sure Francis, I'd write back if somebody wrote me." I look down and smile; we go on sweeping. I don't want to say anymore, because he might change his mind. I have what I want. It's like a shiny, smooth stone in my pocket. Almost any time of the day I can touch it and feel the warmth.

The morning of the last day before summer vacation finally comes. Most of us are sitting outside on the porch, our suitcases piled up. The steamy June sun heats up the smell of the shallow duck pond and mixes it with the green smell of newly mown grass. We are all getting ready to scatter; some guys will just disappear forever. We joke around a lot to cover this up. As usual Bernie lounges at the center of everybody. This will be my last chance to be with him for two years. I'm making myself as inconspicuously, conspicuous as I can.

Then Bernie gets up and goes over to a freshman and asks him to go for a walk. The freshman is short and very athletic. He looks innocent, like he never really had to try hard. I don't feel angry, just disappointed as I watch Bernie walk out of my life with another person. It even makes sense to me that he would pick someone real cute. As I turn away and say goodbye to Johnny that little voice inside says, "Some day, he'll want to walk with you."

Chapter 14

This summer, no one even mentions camping trips. Dick is at officers' training school; mom and dad are beginning to get worried about trouble in a country called Vietnam. As for Chris, mom knows one of the secretaries who works at his high school. This secretary casually mentioned to mom that Chris just stands all alone between classes, not even embarrassed looking, just distant. I try not to think about this too much. With Dick gone, Chris and I even have separate rooms. What with how busy I am, I don't see much of him. He spends most of the summer in his room.

Mom and dad are about the same, dad picking me up, mom keeping things running. I start getting acne fairly bad at this time. Being skinny and having acne in a regular high school might be scary but to me it's just a kind of penance, a sign that being attractive and sexual are not what I'm supposed to be about.

In St. Paul I go to Mass every week. Even though I go with my family I know that some day I'll be up on that altar performing the Mass really separated from them. Priests are separated from almost everybody by a kind of awesomeness. Their insides aren't important, only what they represent stands out. Even when they're not performing Mass, people are so respectful that they start looking uncomfortable when priests even come into the room. It's not that I want people to be uncomfortable around me, I just don't want people to investigate too closely what goes on inside. Even telling Fr. Ford about being attracted to men, I still live in a secret place I need to protect. It's almost like that secret place is me. In the priesthood this separation from everybody is repaid by some mysterious closeness with God.

When priests perform Mass they become intermediaries between people and God. With such an important and awesome function, their humanness is not quite so important or even relevant. All this mystery and secretness climax during the part of the Mass called the Consecration. By the time the Consecration takes place the priest has already spent about twenty minutes up on the altar praying while the altar boys occasionally join in and perform various strategic functions like ringing bells and moving the bible from one side of the altar to the other side and most importantly bringing the priest cruets of wine and water. The priest washes his hands with the water and then time kind of slows down.

Things are supposed to run very smoothly. Dick and I used to be altar boys together and like I said,

Dick is always adverse to things running too smoothly. I would try to fit myself into the solemnity while Dick would be resisting the whole time.

The priest and Dick and I would be all spotlighted on that altar. Hundreds of people including our parents would be quietly shuffling below us in the church. I would be squirming and making funny sounds to get Dick's attention to remind him that we had to bring water and wine to the priest. Everyone in the church would be watching as Dick and I were caught in some desperate conflict that we had been preparing for since birth. Finally the priest broke the spell by turning and shooting us with a sharp, exasperated look, his voice tearing from him in a whisper, "Wine and water, now!" Dick got up like he was going on a spring outing.

I still hate being an altar boy, but still whenever the priest finally gets to the consecration of the Mass even my embarrassment opens up to something mysterious and almost free. He takes a little piece of bread, stares at it for a moment, genuflects, and says, "Take this and eat, for this is My Body, sacrificed for the forgiveness of sins." As an altar boy rings the bells this piece of bread becomes the body of Christ which the priest holds in his trembling hands before eating it. Then he stares at the chalice of wine and says, "Take this and drink, for this is My Blood shed for the forgiveness of sins." The wine in the chalice now becomes the blood of Christ which the priest reverently drinks. The bells are ringing now too. A special hush settles over everybody present. Maybe it's the silence or the bells or that special intense almost inhuman look on the priest's face, but even with my embarrassment I know that I'm in on something strange and important, some final, desperate gesture of kindness so foreign to my private hopes and fears and destiny. But this experience is like a tune that I can never quite remember after Mass.

For the rest of the summer I watch destiny unwind for Chris all the time hoping that I have evaded my own. The priesthood is the name of my future.

Chapter 15

In my third year of the seminary I'm chosen by the faculty to be the head sacristan. Everyone knows now that I'm being specially groomed for success in the world of sanctity. It fits me well. As head sacristan I do the same thing every day in meticulous detail: laying out vestments for eight priests, first the white starched surpluses, then the satin chasubles that change color with the ecclesiastical seasons; lighting and extinguishing candles; filling incense containers; pouring wine and water into crystal cruets; and finally making absolutely sure that there are enough tiny hosts of bread to be consecrated as the Body of Christ so that all the seminarians present can partake of this feast.

I guess it's because I guard against accidents so thoroughly that I excel at repetitious detail. Some of my urgency of being a spy is replaced by being very, very careful. This gives me a fighting chance to have a life here. Because I am so successful at not sinning, I'm only at the mercy of accidents. Accidents rend the fabric of my routine leaving me naked and vulnerable. Even though someone must be punished after an accident, accidents seem to occur pretty randomly. I can't always catch them ahead of time.

Shortly after I get back to school I spend my opportunity to write Bernie a letter. It doesn't say much because there's so much I can't begin to tell him.

"Hi Bernie,

How are you? Do you like Washington? Everything here is going fine. I'm head sacristan this year. It's hard work, but I like it. Studies are about the same except I'm not very good at physics. I lost a few classmates last summer.

I hope that everything is going well for you. I miss you. Sometimes when I'm out on the porch and there's a bunch of guys together laughing, I imagine you in the middle of them just sitting and taking it all in. Then I look more carefully and know you're not there.

Sincerely Yours,

Francis Meyers" To which, I didn't get an immediate response, although even I could tell it wasn't much of a letter.

On December 15, I get a card from Washington. This is another kind of accident. For a few moments I don't care about being perfect, I only know that Bernie wrote to me. The front of the card is a deep opaque red, embossed on it are golden silhouettes of Mary, Joseph, and the Baby Jesus, like golden shadows.

"Hi Chris,

Thanks for your letter, I enjoyed hearing from you. Washington is fine. I hope your new year will be full of peace and contentment.

Sincerely Also,
Bernie McQuade"

For a couple of weeks I savor, "I enjoyed hearing from you." Once and a while I even take the card out of my desk and feel his signature with my fingers. Then the routine of the seminary moves on, but with Bernie I can never forget everything. You see I spin in two different orbits: one around the seminary and one around Bernie. These orbits don't morally contradictory each other because I've trained myself not to be sexual. These orbits help me stay alert because there is kind of contrast between them. This creates an element of surprise in my life; I can switch orbits. A word, a card, or even a memory brings me back to Bernie's orbit, accidents bring me back to the seminary.

Chapter 16

Every few days the priest consecrates a special, large covered chalice called the ciborium. This contains hundreds of tiny hosts that become the Body of Christ. Since I am very careful, I ask the priest every couple of days if there are enough hosts to give out to all the seminarians for the following day. During one Mass just when I'm feeling a little wonderful after the consecration I see the priest, Fr. Roberts, open the ciborium getting ready to serve us our hosts. He looks into the ciborium, appears stunned, peers back into the ciborium and mutters something while his face pinches up in that particularly ominous way of his. He then starts breaking each tiny wafer into double, triple, and quadruple pieces. Like a sentence handed down from on high, I realize that there are not enough hosts. I know I asked the priest the day before if there were enough hosts. He said yes. Like something terrible and sudden that has already happened before you're aware of it, I know an accident has just occurred and I am its center. I try to turn the clock back so I can fix whatever went wrong. But I never get a foothold in the past long enough to change it. Finally my sanctified identity lies in rubble at my feet and all that is left is me trying to be invisible again. I want to hide behind that television set in my family's living room, a hidden witness who may never come out. But here I am listening to that breaking sound of hosts and the uneasy shuffling of kneeling seminarians.

We all know around here that painful accidents reveal unworthiness. They're somebody's fault; definitely within someone's moral control. The true Francis, who's even more careless than Dick stands out. If I were really good this wouldn't happen to me, but to other people.

Gentle Jesus seems totally irrelevant; something deeper and older lifts its head. Fr. Roberts emits a kind of hissing sound like steaming radiators; his face is flushed and dangerous. This time I'm the target of what feels like eternal punishment, and I'm aware that now my failure confirms everyone else's perfection. After all we are trained to be survivors here.

The force that holds me orbiting safely around the seminary trembles; I am thrust out. I struggle to find a new orbit before I am spun off into the chaos of my lone destiny. Figuring things out is irrelevant to that desperate attempt to wrench myself back into the safety of a future in the seminary. The darkness where I spin out into is deeper than words; it's a place out of which I rose and to which I will return.

In the midst of all this hiding and scrambling

terror something strange then happens, not a solution which is what I really want, but a little unimportant idea pops up kind of out of nowhere…maybe I can tell somebody about this, not like in the confessional because telling now can't save me. It's just I want to talk about what's happening, and I don't even know why. That's when this little marker bobs up in the screaming panic almost like a cork. That corks marks the spot of whatever is happening, so at least I can remember it.

I don't understand this accident stuff when I'm actually in the middle of it; it's too confusing and I don't want it to be happening, but at least I can remember…I look around for someone with whom I can talk. Someone I'm not afraid of. I think of my classmates. In my junior year there are only five of us left out of a class of twenty five. Bob Greco quit last summer. He kept getting quieter and quieter. Last summer he wouldn't leave his family's home even for church. His mother called in a special doctor who said Bob shouldn't go back to the seminary. At least this is what Mario said who lives nearby. I don't want to talk with Mario either. We never did talk too much and mostly just reassured each other by going on walks. Besides this past summer transformed him from a shy little boy into a deep voiced, strong looking Italian man. He's changing so fast I'm not sure what to make of him. Besides I saw him with his shirt off yesterday and I have to be careful not to look at him too closely so I don't have impure thoughts. It wouldn't be good talking to Gene either. I can just see his round shaking body and hear that loud laughter; I'd wonder if he was laughing at me. It wouldn't work with Tim either. I think that he wants to be more perfect than I am. Even though he's so smart, the priests chose me to be sacristan. He's started asking me about my test scores. Besides he has enough of his own problems. Fr. Roberts has started to say that Tim has no soul. Tim laughs like he's just been given a complement but then afterwards becomes limp, grinds his finger frantically into his nose, and studies harder.

I decide on Johnny. So many dramatic things have happened to me here that sometimes I forget about when we walked around the pond and talked about his eyes. He's always been in the background though, ready to look at me head on and be curious in a friendly way about what's going on with me. He'd be a good person to help me mark that scary accident stuff.

I ask Johnny to go on a walk for this purpose. It's a chilly and damp November afternoon. The ducks are squawking.

As usual he seems comfortable and friendly. Unlike Mario, he hasn't grown much taller.

Walking, I sort of build my courage to talk. Then I jump in. "Johnny, I felt so crummy about what happened with the hosts and Fr. Roberts…I was so scared during it. I just haven't quite gotten over the feeling. It wasn't my fault. I asked the priest the day before and he said that there were enough hosts. Fr.

Roberts didn't even want to hear about that, he was just mad. I couldn't prevent it from happening. If this happens to me once, it'll happen again, no matter how hard I try."

Our steps squish in time through the slimy leaves. It's funny how when you walk with someone you your steps become in sync almost like a dance. Then he starts, "I've been wondering what's been going on Francis, you look pretty quiet lately. I was almost going to ask you, but you seem pretty private." Our steps move in a squishy rhythm. "That really was a tough break, Francis. I decided not to go to communion that day so things wouldn't be worse for you."

"But it's just not fair; it's not fair!"

Johnny appears kind of stumped, but after we walk silently for a couple of minutes he says, "I suppose it's not fair, but sometimes things just happen, like my eyes and I just have to make the best of it. These things happen to all of us no matter how hard we try. It just feels real bad for a while." He stops for a moment and looks at me straight forward like he has to, because of his eye condition.

"God, it was horrible!"

He just kind of takes in my feelings for a minute and then he starts in. "Francis you're walking with me right now and I'm glad to be your friend."

Not being sure exactly what a friendship is, I decide that probably this might be it. Our steps continue to make a duet of squishing sound. Things don't seem quite so bad; somehow marking that frightening moment with Johnny makes it a little smaller, not smaller exactly; maybe the feeling is just set into something, like there's a background. But still once and a while now when there's a sudden crash in my vicinity and I notice I'm not the center of it, right before I feel relieved that I'm not involved and someone else is to blame, I can hear those hosts breaking…

Chapter 17

A screaming squeal of car tires braking on the road outside, pierces the closed apartment. Francis opens his eyes reluctantly, the bubble of memory bursting. Francis stares out at the alien present moment in which he has been so rudely deposited. Breathing shallowly he cautiously lifts his head and then shoulders, propping himself up by his elbows, searching for some familiar landmark. His eyes settle on the plants in the window. A deep breath fills his lungs. The startled look on his face softens as he focuses ever more intently on the twining tendrils of the plant filling the window. He glances toward the clock at his bedside, tick, tick, tick, an eternity of mechanical predictability, and he a reluctant foolish virgin who fell asleep and missed her chance for heaven.

Even at his most pious, Francis never measured up to those virgin martyrs staring out of the gold edged holy cards that he saved while normal boys his age saved baseball cards. The haloed girls standing next to implements that were used to torture them, stared serenely out at Frances. St. Lucy refused to marry a pagan; her eyes were gauged out before she was killed. Now she is the patroness of light. St. Apollonia refused to denounce her faith; her teeth were pulled out before she was murdered. She is the patroness of dentists. St. Barbara, faithful to Christ, was chained to a chariot wheel and burned to death. She is the saint soldiers. They seemed so willing and unafraid, their eyes frozen with numbed innocent devotion. They knew that they didn't deserve their pain. Someone else's evil brought them to this predicament, no blame for them, the bliss of innocence was all ready transporting them to God's bosom, that cool changeless lap of ecstasy free from any hint of accident.

Perhaps if Francis tried a little harder…

He squints at the clock, 11:30. He's forgetting something. He knows the feeling of some accident brewing, some oversight, something he should have known, if only he had… He takes a sharp little in breath. Chris, Chris, he's got to get back to Chris. He'll think something is wrong and spend all night imagining terrible scenarios in which innocent Francis might be caught… innocent. Francis smiles grimly. His fingers punch the familiar numbers on the phone. He presses the receiver to his face listening intently. The ringing in his ear abruptly stops.

"Hello?" Chris has been waiting by the phone.

"Hi Chris, it's Francis, How are you?"

There's a pause, the slower, deeper voice begins.

"I'm doing fine this week. I was wondering if you wanted to go to breakfast tomorrow morning."

Pausing as if pleasantly surprised by the invitation, Francis answers, "Sure, Chris, that sounds great. How about 9:30?"

Francis smiles softly. "Well, I'll see you tomorrow."

After another pause, "That sounds good Francis."

Francis slowly lowers the phone, another accident avoided. Chris is safe. This fragile moment is all right, all right. Lights still on, he lies back on his bed, eyes open but not looking out, his memory again taking charge. What he could have done or shouldn't have done disappears in a maze.

Chapter 18

None of us here in the seminary think too deeply about our relationships, even animosities run shallow; the seminary runs deep. We all have to get along but hope the people we don't like disappear. Survival is always the best revenge. Johnny, Tim, Gene, Mario, and myself all come back for the fourth year. I am comfortable with this arrangement. We are in good hands.

The priests here are responsible for how we turn out during these four years at Mary Valley. Then they pass us on to a new group of priests in Washington, who will continue perfecting us during the two years there. After this we take our first vows of poverty, chastity, and obedience; we become real members of this religious order, although we're still several years short of actually being ordained as priests. But even during my fourth year I see more clearly how everything here drives us to that final destination. Obedience is the engine.

Even the amount of food we get figures into the

scheme of things. There is a hierarchy, starting with God and working its way down to us. The priests are pretty high in the scheme of things. They get different food from us; it looks and smells wonderful. Since they are not seminarians, they can actually choose what they want to eat for their meals, things like stuffed pork chops and roast chicken.

Since we seminarians are considerably further down the hierarchy, our fare is more humble. This makes sense to me. Sometimes Fr. Harte encourages us by saying that he looks forward to the day that we too can join what he calls the club and eat at the priests' bounteous table. My classmates and myself are encouraged by the news that we will have more to eat in Washington next year.

Johnny is about the same, but I notice him a little more. He's real friendly but he doesn't stick to people. At least that's what I call it. Almost everybody here sticks together. If you find someone you feel safe with, you hold on for dear life. Most of us also stick to the seminary. The longer we're here, the harder we stick. It's so funny because Johnny doesn't stick to anybody but he's my friend. He's not too busy sticking, to listen.

Tim sticks to studying. During free time Tim can usually be found hunched over a book in study hall, his head bobbing urgently as he memorizes things. Gene sticks to a junior named Tony. Tony is strong and athletic looking. Gene knows enough how things work here and watches his step. Even though he laughs loudly as if he doesn't have a care in the world, he watches carefully so that he doesn't cross a line. Mario continues to become more handsome. We talk and walk sometimes, but I end out thinking about the hair that is growing on his chest. It's hard to be friends with someone when that is all you can think about.

Gene notices when Mario and I walk together. I think he wants to get to know Mario, but Mario is shy of Gene.

Mario introduced me to his father last week during a visiting Sunday. Once a month we can get visitors here, although my family lives too far away to come. Mario his father and me were walking around the playing field; the track hurdles were still set up. Mario asked his father if he knew how to run them.

"Sure son, I used to be a track star in high school."

"You said you were a track star, come on dad, show me." Mario looks very proud.

"I don't know son, it's been a while."

"Please dad?"

And off Mario's father went, this man who looked pretty old to me, running and kind of hopping over the hurdles. Mario watched very quietly like something pretty terrible was happening inside. Later that day he came up to me, "My dad jumps hurdles like a girl, as if he expected his dad to be wonderful. Maybe that's why Mario seems vulnerable to me, he still gets hurt when things turn out to be not as wonderful as he thinks they should be.

Besides Mario is getting pretty complicated, especially around sex. Between junior and senior years he has really started to notice girls. Mostly Mario and I get along pretty well, in spite of his new magnificence. We are both friends of Johnny.

Almost as if it's a reward, at the beginning of the year I'm given one of the most important jobs in the seminary: cleaning the priests' recreation room. I have always had a hard time imagining what they do up there. Even when I catch a glimpse of them with regular clothes on instead of cassocks, they have so much power over me that they seem like mysterious aliens.

But now every morning I walk up the stairs of the old resort building and open the door into the secret chamber where priests spend their evenings together having fun. The room smells of cigarette smoke. There's dingy furniture, a new TV set, some magazines, cigarette butts, and partially empty glasses. The bottoms of the glasses the morning after are coated with variously colored sticky skins that haven't managed to completely dry out yet. The glasses sit abandoned on tables around the room.

First I empty ash trays and then collect the glasses, putting them in a small sink. Then I rub the colored skins out of the bottoms of the glasses under a stream of warm water, drying and placing them back in a cupboard. Finally I wipe off all the table surfaces with a damp cloth. My job is to tidy things up but more importantly not to say anything about what I see there. I am becoming the guardian of their mystery. The priests know that I will be careful. I overheard

Gene telling Tim that he, Tim, should have gotten this job since he has better grades.

This is about the time that Vince, that guy who works here, disappears. After those first few days at Mary Valley I didn't see him much. We seminarians are on a real tight schedule. Sometimes though, I would see him standing at a distance watching us as we filed by. I could never tell if it was a tender or angry look on his face. Gene, who knows just about everything that goes on here, said with excitement that Vince tried to kiss a freshman in the laundry room. I know, especially because of my experience with Bud, that Vince should never have done that. But I wonder if anybody ever cared about him. I remember about him being an orphan and how he sang "Love Me Tender, Love Me True" at that bonfire three years ago.

My senior year is really smooth sailing, except for something very confusing toward the end. But by that time I have already been chosen as valedictorian. Mary Valley is a little different than other schools. The valedictorian is chosen not so much for grades as for other less tangible reasons. I am also picked as prefect of the school for the last semester. I'm kind of a star here. The prefect stands in the awesome position of being responsible to help everybody in the school maintain obedience.

Now I know I'm progressing quite admirably in this life I chose years ago. I can barely remember my last accident. I know that if I try my best to do the right thing, life falls into place. Any casualties are part of a divine scheme which I can trust as long as I impeccably maintain it.

It's at about this time during the apex of my career in sanctity that Gene comes up to me, "Tim and I are having special graduation cards made. Our families are going to pay for them. They're going to be the best!" He laughs in that rolling way.

"Boy Gene, does it cost a lot of money?"

"About fifty bucks, but everybody is coming to see me graduate, my whole neighborhood. Anybody coming out to see you Francis?"

"Oh, I think my mom might be able to fly out."

"Wait till you see all the people I'm inviting." Then he walks away laughing.

A couple of days later in Latin class, Fr. Roberts starts talking about graduation. This event is his pet project. He mentions that he is having special invitations made that we can send out to our guests. Gene raises his hand, "What if some of us want to buy our own special invitations?"

Fr. Roberts shifts his vague black form and shoots a sharp look at Gene and says, "No!" Gene squirms for a moment penetrated by that gaze and then nods his head without laughing.

A few days later Gene comes up to me, "Tim and I are still going to buy our own invitations. You'll see, they'll be terrific!"

"Gene, Fr. Roberts said that you can't do that. You're not supposed to."

"We're gonna do it anyway and they're gonna be

the best, you'll see and I'm gonna have lots of people there. Everybody wants to come to see me." And he sets off laughing about something that clearly I am not in on.

I don't know what to do. I am the prefect now and it's my job to keep other students in line. Reporting infractions of the rule is the hardest thing for me to do because I want everybody to like me. I suppose it'll get easier when I get further along towards the priesthood. Most of the time I walk a fine line between looking strict and not reporting people. I can usually blur things a little bit. This may be my strongest talent.

I don't understand why Gene did this, my dilemma is absolute. I either don't report clear disobedience or I do; no middle ground. I talk with Johnny and Mario; they're not sure what I should do either. I even pray, but I just come up against this cold wall of fear. No answer comes from anywhere so one day I take a running start and do my duty. I need to maintain obedience. This is a very important test for me, an initiation. Hardly breathing I walk up to the room of Fr. Roberts for the first time in my life. Things kind of move by, like I'm on a bus again. My hand knocks on the door.

"Come in," he says in a real friendly way.

I open the door to see him sitting behind his very orderly desk, pink skinned and innocent looking, relaxed like a regular person. This'll be alright, I just know it.

"Father, there is something, I need to tell you."

His soft face becomes menacing like some horror movie transformation. His voice fills the room. "What's happened?"

It's like jumping into a cold pool of water. There is never a moment where you really want to do it, but my running momentum hurls me into mid-air, no choice now, "Father, Gene and Tim are having their own invitations made."

I see an explosion take place in his eyes barely held back by his rigid face, but I know a projectile has been set in motion; I know that I'm the one who aimed it. I want to stop and back up through my memory and do something else. But something keeps dragging me back to this angry man who's going to hurt people. This time I have done it to them.

"I TOLD THEM THAT I WAS DOING THE INVITATIONS!"

I try to step out of the center of the accident, "I don't want to get them in trouble, but I thought I had to tell you."

With eyes focusing on some future punishment he says blankly, "You've done the right thing."

It feels like a nightmare except that I'm the monster. I leave the room. My face is prickly with heat and I am fading in and out of a new kind of embarrassment that's even deeper than before because I have set this accident in motion.

I wait for the aftermath. Obedience, Obedience, Obedience… the kid who went to eternal damnation for disobedience. How come it doesn't fit? I obeyed and it doesn't fit. Me, myself and I did it. Tim and Gene hate me know.

In the evening I see Gene and Tim walking together with a slower than usual pace, talking in whispers. I'm walking with Mario. They both look at me with hostility and fear as they pass. I feel ashamed. As Mario and I walk on, he says unconvincingly, "You had to do it." For the next couple of weeks I try to let the seminary cover up this event, but an edge still slips out. At the very peak of my accomplishment, there's something out of place, something that makes me regret and wonder. It's like forgetting isn't quite enough anymore.

I go through my last pale, misty May at Mary Valley, graduation and summer just beyond. For some reason no matter how hard I try, I can't memorize my valedictory. Fr. Ford, keeping a watchful eye on me, notices my increasing distraction. I still see him every month for spiritual direction. He listens to me tensely, but I don't have much to say anymore. I've learned how to control myself and know how to stop my thoughts and feelings about sexual things before they become sins. Once and a while I can show Johnny an edge of what is going on but pretty much I'm still a spy. I guess that's what being obedient is all about.

During my last session with Fr. Ford he gazes at me almost like he's pleading, or maybe this is how he says goodbye. His face is resting in his large hand. He kind of peeks out of the confines of his strong fingers like his eyes want to escape. He reminds me of those times when I was a kid and would catch butterflies and hold them too tightly only to find broken wings and powder in my grip. As we talk I can almost see shreds of color showing through his tensed hands.

"Francis, how's your valedictory coming along?"

"Oh father, I just can't seem to remember it no matter how hard I try."

His hand over his face clutches even harder and he laughs with tight reassurance. "You'll do us proud, I know it. You can do it, you can do it."

"Father I just can't seem to remember anything!"

Something flutters softly in his eyes. For a moment he looks sad and bewildered, almost like my real father. A little under his breath and looking at me sideways, he says, "You can use index cards Francis, it's all right." Then he switches back to a tight embarrassed laugh, and I know our time together is over. We never talk to each other alone after that, ever again.

Johnny is salutatorian and taking it in stride, thinking about it some, writing it down, and most of all, remembering it. I feel a little funny that he is not valedictorian. I know that he not only gets better grades than I do, but he's more intelligent too. You see, he doesn't compare himself to other people as much as I do.

All of us in my class except Johnny seem like we're driven by something that makes us try real hard; just like Tim with grades. Like we all need something so badly that it hurts and then the trying to get that something makes us lonely. Sometimes lately I've been wondering if the priests are like that too, even Fr. Roberts.

The actual graduation ceremony is pretty routine I suppose. My mother's out in the audience though. Dad scraped up enough money to send her out here. It's funny all those times he drove me out to the bus station blindly hoping everything would be all right; now when everything is finally all right he can't be here. There really wasn't enough money for them both to come out. And driving, he hates driving. He gets afraid, then he gets ashamed he's afraid, and then picks a fight with my mother, who never did have a great capacity to deal with his mistakes.

My mother is another story. Even though this is my success, and I put everything I had into it; when I see her sitting in the audience, I realize it's her idea. Something that she decided when the enemy troops were at the gate. With frantic hope, she passed one of her children on to something that seemed like safety. People say we look a like.

Fr. Roberts welcomes everybody to the graduation. He looks pink and genial like some harmless uncle. Then Johnny gets up and talks his salutatory as if he were walking around the pond with everyone; not dramatic, slightly matter of fact and true. While Fr. Delvechia gives out awards for the highest grades in different classes I can smell the tobacco smoke in his cassock and wonder if he has lighted up in church lately. Tim and Johnny are tied with the most awards,

I come in third. My stomach is flipping over every few seconds…my turn soon.

It's time; everything is very quiet and frozen except for my heart pounding in my ears. I jerkily creep toward the podium holding on to my index cards. They're the important thing. I have to get them onto the podium and then I'll be safe…mission accomplished. I transfer myself to my cards. First card, second card; people don't realize it, but it's the cards, not me speaking. The last card turns over; it's finished. I'm standing looking out blankly for a second and walk back to my seat. I hear clapping, and for a moment I am disappointed that I missed the whole thing. Mostly though it's just over.

After all those years of leaving her managing the kitchen, I can finally rush to my mother.

"Oh, Francis, I'm so proud of you. I just knew you could do it. Fr. Ford said that you gave a better sermon than a lot of priests."

"Boy, mom, was I nervous!"

"You looked like you belonged up there."

We hug; I think she was nervous too; she's shaking slightly, but nobody can tell but me.

From her arms I look up; the whole production is dispersing around us. Johnny, Mario, Tim, Gene are already forgetting about this afternoon, going off with their families. On this day we still belong to parents.

Chapter 19

Summer at home goes by very quietly. Having been valedictorian, I'm really a celebrity around here now. Grandparents, aunts, uncles all stand in distant awe of my accomplishment. I'm not like other people now; people expect me to be separate and watching. Both Dick and Chris are gone. Dick didn't complete officers' training school, so he's in the infantry in Vietnam where a lot of fighting is going on. He sent back pictures of himself standing in front of some sort of theme park in Hong Kong. He's very tan, thin, and smiling in a bruised sort of way. He says he's doing fine. We're all holding our breaths.

Chris is in the navy in Seattle. He didn't say much about it to anyone before he left. In fact during the last couple of years he hasn't said much about anything to anybody. He'd mostly spend time in his room with the shades pulled, sitting in the dark. When he was younger he used to read and write a lot. With it so dark in his room, I'm not sure what he was doing in there towards the end. But I have my life in the seminary to think about. Now I am the only sure thing that my parents have.

It's a quiet summer. Mostly I wonder about next year. My parents don't say much; it's almost like they're holding their breaths, waiting for something beyond their imagination to happen. In September my dad brings me to the bus station again. When my bus roles away, it's almost like he's going into the unknown, not me.

It's the usual trip back but with a new twist, the bus in Chicago says "Washington DC." I know the food is supposed to be better and Bernie's there like a promise. But change always unnerves me. The smallest, most optimistic variation can lead to unpredictable accidents. I know. Still things sound pretty good; more food, more free time, and I finally get to wear a cassock. The cassock part is a saving grace. Almost like a dramatic initiation in the last two weeks, my shoulders, back, and face have broken out with fierce, raspberry swellings; the kind that remain angry and refuse to develop into reassuring white peaks. The cassock's yards of black cloth, buttoned from my starched white collar down to the hem out of which the toes of my shoes peek; serve as an apology. It announces before anybody has time to notice that I have no illusions about anyone wanting anything more than kindness from me. The fact that Washington is hot and humid adds a slightly penitential aspect to it all. I like that.

In Washington the fifth and sixth year men like

myself live in a two story brick building that looks a little like an elementary school. It's set on a fairly busy street on the edge of Catholic University. To the south side lies a lawn area reassuringly too small to be a sports field. To the east, scrubby bushes that turn out to be wild rhododendrons fill a hilly patch of land. In the middle of this scrubby area stands another placid, life sized statue of Mary now relegated to the wilderness. Bernie lives in what's called the major seminary which is only a couple of blocks away from my seminary, the minor seminary. Bernie finished his year in the novitiate in my junior year. This is a place that seminarians go after the second year of college. All year you pray and meditate and finally take vows of poverty, chastity, and obedience. He has been at the major seminary for one year now. I have not heard from him since that Christmas card. I was not deeply disappointed; what would someone like Bernie want from someone like me?

Entering the front door my seminary, I run into Mario who's pretending like he isn't waiting. Funny how embarrassing it is to see familiar people in different settings. I don't know the ground rules yet.

"Hi, Francis."

"Hi, Mario."

"How was summer?"

"Summer was fine."

"How was yours?"

"Pretty good."

"Who's your room mate?"

"I don't know, is there a list posted?"

"Yeah, it's on the bulletin board in the hallway."

"Thank a lot."

"See you later."

"See you later."

We both crawl back into our skins as I turn and head to the bulletin board.

I read the room list. I'm sharing a room with Tom Kelly; a scary chord strikes. I wonder if he still blames me for that D he got. I'm relieved that he's not in, but there's a pile of clothes sitting ominously on his bed. My inner voice softly warns me that I'm not at Mary Valley anymore, as if I hadn't figured that out already. Tim drops in smiling and drilling his nose saying how wonderful Washington is going to be. I tense up without letting him know and then look up and smile at him while still unpacking.

Tom Kelly walks in with the assurance of someone who has been here for a year and is doing fine. "Hi Tim, and, ah, Francis, so your my roommate?" His hands arc on his hips and he's kind of appraising me.

"Ya, um, Tom, good to see you again." I turn around pretending that there's some urgent need to finish putting my underwear in a drawer.

"Tim, good to see you, let me show you around. You'll love this place. Catch you later, roomie."

Now feuds are dangerous here; we live too closely together. Any outspoken animosity disturbs the whole equilibrium, but a lot can go on between the lines that can get pretty bad. I've seen it. Guys just start agreeing that somebody is a jerk. No one needs to say too much. The person gets frozen out. It's funny how I've never felt it from this side before.

Blurring my eyes and blanking out for a minute helps me find a place away from everything, like a little vacation. Finally throwing the rest of my stuff in the drawer, I finally jump into my new world and set out to explore it.

In the seminary people don't like to be caught standing alone, unless you're clearly waiting for something important to happen like an appointment with a priest. There are not many gaps between things and if you get caught in one by somebody you try to pretend that it didn't happen. But in spite of that unstated rule there is usually one place in the seminary where you can stand alone for a while without arousing suspicion. Guys are just drawn to this island of temporary options. I can tell here it's the front yard. You can duck into a sort of open porch, and still be close to the traffic sounds of the world. Dusk has started to settle in, and I'm getting the lay of the land.

I slip into the shadowy talking forms in the front yard and look up. Maybe it's my imagination, but Bernie's there, spotlighted, looking like he's waiting for someone. He catches my glance and smiles a smile so big that it can hold all me hopes. Then I wonder if he's actually looking at me. Quickly I drop my head down in case he's actually pointing his attention at someone behind me. I look up again, just to test, and he's still there stalking my gaze.

His voice calls out to my like we're actually familiar. "Well kid, how was your trip?"

"Um…hi Bernie." I catch the cue to stand next to him.

"I heard great stuff about you last year, your valedictory wowed them."

"Aw, thanks." Even though I still can't say much around him, I can tell by the way he's leaning toward me and sounding real confidential that he's not going anywhere for at least awhile. He has a way of fixing his eyes on a person and just enveloping him in tenderness and then pulling back like it's all a joke, but a kind of tender-sad joke. The thing is, it's not just his eyes but his whole compact body that establishes a connection. He's shorter than me now, but I have this sensation of looking up to him. For a couple of minutes everything is absolutely simple for me inside and outside; I just need to keep my feet planted and feel Bernie next to me. I suppose that there might be happier people somewhere, but for the first time in my life I don't need to compare myself with them.

"Has anyone shown you around town yet?"

"Ah, ah, no."

"I'll do the honors." He bows with a slight flourish and stares at me with softness entwined with irony like some romantic pirate. "You can invite a couple of your classmates and we'll see the sights."

Just then Johnny steps into our light. Things

start feeling pretty complicated again. Not moving and being happy aren't enough. I need to set up a plan with Bernie in which I actually have to include other people. At the same time I have to say hello to Johnny. I hate doing two things at the same time, I can't be careful enough and somebody may see behind the scenes. Johnny would understand, but if I stay confused too long Bernie might think that I don't want to go with him. I come across a brilliant solution, "Hi Johnny, Bernie said he'll show us around Washington. Do you want to come?"

"Sure Francis sounds like fun. How are you doing?"

"Oh, pretty good." And for once I mean it.

Just then Tim walks by and wants to get in on it too. I invite him, too. All the time Bernie's just hovering over me. My inner voice keeps reassuring me, "Keeping moving, don't try to figure it out just keep moving." And I do. Finally it's all arranged. After glances and words bounce back and forth between the four of us on this night of promise, Tim finally says it's time for benediction and we should go in now. For once I've lost track of time.

Before Bernie sets off into the darkness, he taps my shoe with his, "Hey kid, I'll see you guys Sunday about 1PM."

Chapter 20

Benediction is a solemn little event that happens every Sunday afternoon right before supper. We file into the chapel, candles lit, organ playing and incense burning. It feels good to be doing things in a group again; it gives me privacy to take in the whole thing with Bernie. His little tap on my shoe knocked something loose. When I felt that gentle impact things like obedience and being safe kind of shifted almost beyond my vision. Just being there next to Bernie felt like entering a doorway into green fields covered with flowers. Something like joy bubbles up inside a hidden spring that I never noticed before. Myself and the world are all mixed up in some strange and wonderful way that makes this moment of being alive an endless space I fill and then disappear into, like incense.

As the priest enters the sanctuary dressed in a golden cape and steps up to the altar sprinkling incense on glowing coals in the censer, I'm not trying to figure out what I need to do next. The smoky sweet smell of incense touches my heart and I expand into the room. When the priest places the tiny host into a glass case at the center of the large golden rayed monstrance and we all focus our attention on this one sacred spot; I focus too but still keep expanding even beyond the confines of this room into the night sky. I can focus, but all the while my being spreads like a wind of sound and color. Like those comic books taken from Chris and torn into the wind so long ago, the shreds of my life spin and rush by in a river of color, except now I feel ecstasy and not terror. Wondering about Tom Kelly and how I'll fit in here seem meaningless in all this rushing space. As the altar bells shimmer and the priest raises the monstrance to bless us, I feel grace. Sure Bernie's part of it, but it's even bigger than that, something pervasive and invisible like air that you don't even know is there until a breeze brushes your face.

Then it's over; we march out into the more ordinary life of the new seminary. I'm back to normal size glancing protectively around me. But I remember.

The changes here are difficult, but I've been in difficult places before. We meet with Fr. Marquand, the superior here, right after benediction. He is a priest in his fifties with no hair of any sort on his head. He laughs loudly like a machine gun, eyes shining like a doll's. They make me wonder if there is anything soft and warm underneath the skull. During the Second World War, he was a chaplain in the Philippines and lost three fingers of his right hand. He doesn't talk about it, almost like he's forgotten. I suppose he's got more urgent things to do like keeping this place going. After all he's the superior.

When all of us fifth and sixth year seminarians are sitting down in a classroom, Fr. Marquand smiles in a glittery kind of way and begins briefing us, "The first point that I want to make clear is that things are going to be very different here. Ha! Ha! Ha! We're going to treat you like adults, not children, and make real men out of you! Any questions?"

Tim raises his hand, "Back in the old seminary we couldn't talk in the evenings after 7:30 PM, Father."

If Fr. Marquand would have had eyebrows they would be lifted now, "We treat you like adults here. You can talk to each other softly until 9:30 PM."

Gene follows suite, "Back in the other seminary we could only leave the grounds twice a month, Father."

Fr. Marquand looks shocked, "Here we really know how to trust you. In the afternoons you can go to the major seminary or even the cafeteria of Catholic University." He points his blank expression at each of us and grins, "That's all for now. You can all go to bed."

As Tom Kelly and I quietly get ready for bed everything seems a little off center, at least off my center. I condense into dread. I remember what I felt at benediction but I'm stuck in a mine field again. Besides I won't see Bernie for a week. It's not just that life is different here. If it means more food and free time I'm all for it, but there's something ominous about the way Fr. Marquand keeps saying "here" as if there is some kind of dramatic punch line encoded. Like there's some kind of battle going on between the two seminaries, and I may be caught in the middle. I yearn for the safety of predictability.

In the next few days I hear most of the other guys talk about the old seminary as if it's stupid and beneath contempt. A year ago these guys acted like Mary Valley was the whole world, and they scrambled to make themselves part of that world. They don't remember now; they don't even remember that they changed their minds. It all makes me wonder if they have insides. Can you even have insides when you don't remember? I don't understand. Maybe it's just me not learning right.

Thinking about Sunday with Bernie, helps me shift a little into thoughts that aren't so confusing. Bernie drops by on Sunday like he said he would, to pick up Johnny, Tim, and me. I wish I could say that I had a wonderful time, but it was just okay. Bernie seemed distracted and slightly irritable, and I've been burned out with stress and diarrhea. We just looked at a bunch of big, blank buildings. It's not that I'm not in love with Bernie, but this time seeing him I didn't feel that rush of freedom, and I just keep being pressed down by the heaviness of the humid still air and my burning fear about my future here. I want to get back to some routine that I can feel good at.

I start an ordinary week trying to catch all the cues of this place. I run into Johnny a lot; that helps.

He never really identified too strongly with the old seminary and doesn't really identify much with this place either. He doesn't sink down and get swallowed up by places. He's too curious. He's a good person to talk with because he has insides and lets you know what he's thinking. Most of all, he remembers. It's like being on a long trip and meeting another person, finding out what he's seen on the road. You can't join up forever with him, but you can have company for a while and get information that may save your life.

Mario spends a lot of time in his room. When he does come downstairs to play cards or go for walks, he talks about a girl he met last summer. She's a model for department store catalogues. Mostly he sounds far away. I can't give him much of a hand. Between struggling to figure out what's going on here, and wondering what's up with Bernie; I loose track of Mario. It's easy to loose his track because he's stopped leaving clues.

Tim floats around in ecstasy. He's the new sacristan and class prefect. The faculty here shines on him; I remember what that's like. Also no one here tells him that he doesn't have a soul. Perhaps he doesn't remember that though. He just absolutely knows that everything the faculty says is the truth. He looks at me very sympathetically, like maybe I'm slow or something. I am beginning to feel a little afraid of him, not because he is consciously vindictive; it's his innocence that I am most afraid of. Afraid of…I wonder if people were afraid of me back at Mary

Hill? I was so sure the priests were right; after all they spoke for God. Now, if the priests at Mary Hill were wrong, how can I assume that the priests here are so right about things? The one thing the priests here and at Mary Hill have in common is that they are sure they're right. Maybe I'm jealous of Tim; but somehow the situation is more complex than that. I used to think that guilt was connected to doing something bad. Now I'm not so sure; it may even be connected somehow to innocence. I'll talk with Johnny about this.

Gene and Tom Kelly have become best friends. Gene's star has also risen. I pretty much loose track of him because he's very busy. Maybe I'm ashamed for reporting him last year, or maybe just afraid because I know that Tom, his best friend despises me. Gene still laughs in the same old way, but when I come around he becomes very quiet. Tom is just very quiet even when we are alone.

Chapter 21

The priests here don't spy on us, they just watch very closely. I notice it with Fr. Marquand first. He seems to enjoy shocking us and then checking for our reactions. Sometimes I get tired out with all the shocks. One day in theology class while laughing he says, "Have any of you noticed that we don't say the rosary here?"

We all nod.

"The rosary is a thing of the past. I know that you said it at that other place, but we are more modern and don't do that here." His eyes peer around at us merrily. Gene is laughing, clearly in on the joke. So far so good, those doll eyes of Fr. Marquand move on. Tim is laughing compliantly and reverently. Satisfied, the eyes move on. Mario is just barely laughing, but since he's been here he's barely laughed at anything. The eyes pass on, placated. Johnny is chuckling, but it's pretty hard to tell what he's chuckling about since he's not looking up. The eyes move on with a hint of reluctance. Then those eyes that seem like glass fix on me, and I can't laugh. I really would try if I could, but I really do like the rosary. When I flew to St. Paul on the plane after graduation I had it in my pocket. When the engines started roaring and my mother and I were pushed back into our seats as the plane lurched forward and started slanting up into the sky barely getting its tail off the ground, I fingered those beads and said Hail Mary's and Our Father's practically the entire trip. We used to say the rosary every afternoon at Mary Valley and that was often the safest part of the day for me, passing my fingers over the smooth beads, repeating prayers, and all the while imagining stories about Jesus and Mary. Sometimes even, the suffering of Jesus touched me and I felt a little more relaxed about painful accidents, not so quick to feel superior to other people. You see by His crucifixion, he took the blame for all our sins and wiped our souls clean. We all get a new start. New starts sound good to me.

I'm thinking about all this, Fr. Marquand is smiling at me not really warmly, "Do you have any problems with this Francis?"

"Um, I don't know; I like the rosary, Father. It's been good for me."

"Ha! Ha! Ha! You would say that! We want you to be men here, not boys. The rosary is a crutch."

"Can't it just be a prayer we say sometimes?"

"I told you that we don't do that here!" He nods in a sharp little motion like he's just checked off something about me.

I know Fr. Marquand is trying to jolt us, maybe

even a little like what happened when Bernie tapped my shoe. But it feels like Fr. Marquand does it by ridiculing and then shoving. My secret voice doesn't like that, although I try my best to go along with Father Marquand. At Mary Hill my inside voice and my outside self had a kind of truce except for when there was an accident. Now my outside self is caught in one accident after another and my inside voice has to take over sometimes just to keep me going.

A priest named Fr. Riley is also on the faculty, teaching Bible Studies. He's from Ireland and seems to be an exile here just like me. Unfortunately I have some trouble with him too. He stands up in front of us with a lost look in his eyes, but there's an edge to his voice that says he's been pushed and shoved too far, and that we better listen and listen carefully. I can tell he's not mean, but he'd just rather shove than be shoved. I think he's forgotten how to be confused. He has very interesting ideas about the Bible.

"Now I want all of you students to understand that the Bible is the word of God. Do you remember how the prophets in the Old Testament predicted the events of the life of Christ?"

We all nod.

"Well, if you look carefully at the New Testament, you can see modern events predicted there also."

My inside voice starts wondering. It's not that Fr. Riley is necessarily wrong, and he is a nice quiet person most of the time; but I wonder what he thinks of Fr. Marquand's modern ideas. I wonder if Fr. Marquand laughs at him too. Just when I'm wondering about this I forget to nod.

"Francis, is this hard for you to understand?"

For a moment I think maybe Fr. Riley wants to actually help me figure this out; so I decide to share my confusion. "Yes it's pretty difficult; no matter how hard I try I just can't see all those dates and events buried in the stories, Father. Last night I kept going over this passage over and over again until I saw all sorts of strange things but nothing that seemed absolutely clear."

His eyes narrowed to a squint and his hands clenched. Maybe he thought I was ridiculing him. Then his face but not his hands opened up and his voice became soft but with a sharp edge underneath. "My son, that's where you have to read with the eyes of faith. If you don't see it, you need to pray to God to open you up. Do you hear me?" Something tells me he's keeping score too.

A priest named Fr. Murphy teaches ethics. He is probably in his mid thirties, tall and stocky with receding but still dramatic black hair. Tim and Gene have taken him as spiritual director and are crazy about him. Fr. Murphy talks like a camp counselor telling stories around a fire late at night. He's not interested in figuring things out as much as inspiring people. He walks into class his cassock swishing dramatically. He gazes up above our heads a little and sighs in relief like he has barely escaped the clutches of some demon and wants to tell us all the dramatic details. When he's not teaching he reads novels about priests who break up spy rings. In his room he has a small fish bowl in which he keeps a large black goldfish who listlessly whirls its extravagant fins in the close confines. I haven't gotten in trouble with Fr. Murphy yet.

John Austen is also on the faculty; he's due to be ordained in two years. He teaches English. He's tall and thin and seems to float into rooms. In spite of his zephyr like appearance, when he looks at you, you know someone is inside. He has a clever, ironic wit that doesn't focus on any specific person, but rather on the more general condition of living. He doesn't herd seminarians the way the priests do. I like him. He's smart and I never can anticipate how he'll respond to a new idea. Maybe things aren't all frozen inside him yet. Most of all he's a saboteur, introducing us to authors who don't believe in happy endings or sometimes even God. He doesn't hit us over the head with ideas; he just plants seeds. Even though I'm seen as old fashioned around here, I can tell he likes me. We talk about ideas and he listens to me with curiosity.

Finally the faculty is rounded off by Fr. Frank Donlevy. He teaches advanced algebra and takes care of the grounds of both seminaries. He eats at our refectory and meets with the faculty weekly; but we really don't see much of him. Unlike everyone else here, he dresses in work cloths and very nonchalantly at that. He wonders in and out of our lives enigmatically and seems to have some sort of a connection to another seminary for high school boys down the street. He gets a lot of young visitors.

Chapter 22

Whenever it gets too hard learning the ropes around here I go up to visit Bernie. I don't actually say I'm going to visit him, people might guess how I feel. I just find some excuse to visit the major seminary where he lives. I find an opportunity about once a week to be in the vicinity of Bernie. While I'm there I'm on a special "Bernie Alert." No matter who I'm talking to or what I'm doing I'm also sounding the waters for him. Like in one of those World War II navy movies where a ship is cruising on the sunlit surface of the ocean, all the while actually sending signals down into the depths, searching. It's really exhausting to be friendly on the surface and desperately, deeply watching at the same time. Fortunately I've had practice being a spy. Maybe that's why some of the guys think I'm spacy.

At first Bernie would single me out sometimes even before I'd get him on my radar. He'd suddenly be by my shoulder, eyes focusing on me. Then he'd lean toward me, and even if we were in a room full of other guys, Bernie and I would be alone. "Well kid, how you doing?"

I'd say, "Oh, ah, pretty good, Bernie," and then become incoherent. He usually then would hover over me for a while. Towards the end of our time together he'd casually touch my shoulder or, like before, tap my shoe; and for another moment I'd be in a universe of excitement where my whole self buzzed with courage and ingenuity. And then it was over. We'd never say much; I suppose a lot of that was me and being so shy around him. He'd notice someone else in the room and say, "Well kid, good to see you, catch you later."

As he'd leave, he'd take my charmed universe with him and I'd be left to fend for myself in the real world of accidents. After several weeks of this one day I go to the major seminary, I get Bernie on my radar and I notice that he's singling out someone else, a guy named Michael. He is a year older than Bernie, very slight and plays the piano beautifully. At first I think that maybe Bernie didn't see me and I'll give him another chance. But each time I come he's singling out Michael. I try to look busy, but not too busy, because I want Bernie to know that I'm still available. One day I finally understand that my days of being singled out by Bernie are over.

My inside voice, maybe to comfort me, lets me in on what it knows. It has been watching Bernie for a long, long time I suppose with my eyes. At Mary Valley Bernie would focus on a guy for a while, and then he'd shift to someone else. I was on the outside then, and didn't notice that there was always an end to the relationship, or at least to the intimate, safe looking part.

Now after focusing on me for a while, Bernie is switching to someone else, but it's not so much about me but rather how Bernie is.

Don't get me wrong about Bernie; he moves in a kind of grace, like a cat that stretches in the sun, its whole body opening and pulling all at the same time in restrained ecstasy. You can almost smell the contentment in its warm fur. Then the cat turns eyes at you and out of shear joy stares and cat-smiles. For a moment you're in the sun too. And then the greeting is over, the cat moves on to another sunny lap.

I understand this sometimes. Other times I fall into a black hole. But the whole process is made a little easier for me because I can tell that I'm now identified as one of Bernie's friends, which is a pretty good thing to be in the seminary. Even though my status with the faculty is getting shaky here, being known as a friend of Bernie's, props me up in some mysterious way. He's pretty powerful around here.

And still every once in a while when I go to the major seminary, I feel his presence and look up to see him stretching in the sun nearby. He smiles at me and says, "How you doing, kid?" Right before he leaves, his shoe taps my shoe, and for a moment I feel a sunny wind on my face.

That Bernie noticed me in the first place was a miracle; I'm tall, skinny, pimply, not athletic, and definitely not brave. But the fact that he adopted me for a while, makes me think that there maybe something interesting inside me. He knows about these things.

Besides I don't want to hurt Bernie just because he doesn't give me what I want. The nice thing about not really believing the priests anymore is that I get a chance to begin to understand what's right for me. Not that I am a theologian or anything, but still I can put a few pieces together. Like, it's a bad thing to try to hurt somebody that you are in love with. In my outer behavior I can forget that rule, but my inside voice gently reminds me. It's at about this time that Bernie starts saying to me, "Your tough as nails, Francis." I may even know what he means.

All this while Johnny and I are becoming better friends. Unlike with Bernie, the relationship happens really gradually like I'm hardly trying. When Johnny smiles I don't get excited. Because I don't have to do anything for Johnny to like me, the different parts of me start coming together like a puzzle finding a picture. Besides I know that Johnny remembers Mary Valley or at least who he was there. I decide that it is time to talk with him about Bernie. I ask him to go for a walk.

Our feet knock along the ground for a while before I start, "You know, Johnny, there's some stuff going on that's pretty hard to talk about; but since we've been talking about things for a while, I thought you ought to know this about me, too."

"Sure Francis, I'm always interested in hearing about what's going on inside you. Heck, we've made it this far."

"Well you see I'm in love with Bernie and all along I've been attracted to men. I haven't done any thing physical, but it just seems to be a pretty steady part of who I am."

"You know I did notice that you were tense around Bernie, but I didn't really think about it." We continue walking the paths in that scrub area with the white statue of Mary in the middle. Johnny just stops, not dramatically, but like he's deep in thought. In the dusk he looks at me straight in the face. "Well Francis, thanks for telling me. The way I look at it, this is just something that's part of you, and heck, you're my friend." Then he laughs in that way of his that makes the world seem interesting.

We start up with our walking again. "You know Francis, I've never told anybody about this, but even though I'm attracted to women, a couple of years ago, I had a wet dream about humping a guy. All of us may be surprising, deep down inside."

We just keep walking around those dark paths barely lighted by the rising moon. Pretty soon we're talking about classes and ideas, and it seems pretty ordinary to me that I'm attracted to men. No tension between inside and outside voices now because I'm just speaking the way trees sprout leaves.

Chapter 23

For a while Bernie is pushed to the outskirts of my mind as I begin stumbling to some new place in seminary life. For the last couple of months or so it's been a joke around here that I cling to outmoded beliefs. The guys here don't seem to remember that they once thought those old fashioned ideas were absolutely right. Now they think that their new fashioned ideas are absolutely right. Can't they keep both absolutes in their minds long enough to see how one replaced the other?

At any rate on Wednesday evening Fr. Murphy teaches a class on ethics; I'm more curious about what makes things right or wrong these days. He's at the blackboard, just having sketched in a diagram that absolutely proves through the theology of St. Thomas Aquinas, that God exists. I'm following him closely maybe even a little urgently, especially after he says that if someone doesn't believe in this line of thought they have some sort of mental problem.

Then Fr. Murphy extends the diagram; scratching

sounds of chalk on the black board sharpen my attention.

"Here you can see that when I extend the diagram from Absolute God, through God's absolute laws, then finally to us; all of our actions, even the tiniest are right or wrong in relationship to God's Absolute Truth. Isn't it marvelously exciting that God dictates what we should do in every moment? All we have to do, is go back to the Absolute and we will know exactly how to act. What wonderful confidence this gives us."

I'm listening carefully, jumping from word to word, meaning to meaning, like stepping stones in a stream. I don't exactly slip, but experience an absolute break, a discontinuity that tumbles me around and then places me back on my seat, except my mouth is hanging open.

Fr. Murphy mistakes my stunned expression for incomprehension. He asks sympathetically, "Francis, do you understand?"

As I'm orienting myself, I say spontaneously, "I do, but it just doesn't apply." Then the spinning in my head stops. There is a strange silent stillness. Then I hear the feet of my classmates shuffling in the room as if I had never heard that sound before; like I'm waking up to that sound, waking a new world that I have fallen into.

I watch sympathy switch to irritation on Fr. Murphy's face. Very slowly he goes over the whole diagram again as if repeating it is an answer, a sing song lullaby that distances himself from me and my new world. "I've gone through this in great detail again; surely the rest of you understand this?" Looking at the other students, Fr. Murphy seems to be reassured. "Do you understand it now, Francis?"

I'm in this new world and naked, I'm trying to find my way back to the world I knew, but back is just blank. "I followed your diagram Father, but, I don't know how to say this exactly, but everything you wrote is just somebody's idea, maybe even a good idea, but still just an idea."

There's a minor explosion inside Fr. Murphy's face. Then he covers it over with deeper layers of icy sympathy. "If some of you are having difficulty with this very complex and important material, you can see your spiritual director. He may be able to help you."

I start trembling now, uncontrollably scrambling for something to cover myself with. A lone hand goes up behind me. It's Johnny, "The ideas of the diagram are clear Father, but how do we know that they are really true?"

"Johnny, your a bright boy, certainly you understand this?" Fr. Murphy looks smiling but there's an icy threat underneath. "It's time now to wind up this class. I am very glad that most of you were able to appreciate this important material." Fr. Murphy fastens an icy sympathetic expression on me and walks out of the room with a dramatic flourish. I here Gene laughing behind me, but what Johnny did was enough; I know that I am not completely alone.

Now there's a fragile point when someone makes a leap, at least someone timid like me. If no one would have understood me at all, I might have actually tried to crawl back into my old self, just to belong. I would have had to cut off that curious part of me. I still couldn't have actually gone back, but I could have buried the new part of me and pretended even harder.

Johnny hears part of what I am saying. I know his voice. Someone knows where I'm at and is interested. I can remain in the land of the living. I wonder how many other people, maybe even some priests, didn't have Johnny in the back of the classroom.

It's not courage. I've never been courageous; compliant and earnest, yes. I hear shuffling in the classroom around me again and feel some kind of new danger. This fear doesn't touch me quite as deeply as before. Burning inside is a new separation; even my senses are ringing. There's life inside that's coming out. I don't know what this means for me, but I've landed somewhere new. This is some kind of doorway.

I'm the last to leave the classroom; it's easier that way. I do know that the first chance I get, I'm going to talk with Johnny and see what he's figuring out. For the time being, I need to be careful.

After this I notice that many of the guys here are beginning to talk to me in a slightly new way. There's a little pause now before they say things to me. I walk in this little ripple of delay, a little pause of silence. I remember that circle of silence back at Mary Hill, except that I was on the other side. I remember.

It's about at this time that Johnny and I start taking long walks at night, talking about God, philosophy, the past, Bernie, and a girl that Johnny met last summer. We wait until everybody is supposed to be in bed. Then we secretly rendezvous at the back door in the basement that nobody uses much, unlock it and set out to parts unknown, figuring things out. We are clearing disobeying the rules. This isn't an accident but a choice. While we walk, the yellowish glow of a Washington night soaks the soft air; stars barely peak through. Even though we are doing this in secret I am slightly aware that there could be very painful consequences for Johnnie and me. I am taking a risk although I won't think about that too much.

My experience in the classroom with Fr. Murphy triggers off a chain of events. A week later my spiritual director, Fr. Bedford, sends me a note.

"Francis, Please see me on Tuesday at 8PM.
Fr. Bedford"

A few weeks earlier, I had chosen him as my spiritual director. He has a reputation for being brilliant and broad minded. Now, it's not that I'm brilliant, but it seems to me that my thinking is spreading out. I'd like a spiritual director with a pretty broad playing field. I might stand a chance at being understood. The fact that Fr. Bedford lives at the major seminary and may not have talked much with the priests here is another factor in my choice. He's a man in his mid fifties with very white hair and a very precise way of speaking. Sometimes when I had been at the major seminary sounding the depths for Bernie I've seen Fr. Bedford pacing the hallways like he's figuring things out. At least that's what I hope.

I walk up to his room Tuesday evening, pretty hopeful. His door is already open; he nods me in, silently pointing to a chair.

He finally cracks open the silence. "I was speaking with Fr. Murphy. He said that you are having some kind of difficulty."

Things have really been difficult for me, and I start thinking that maybe Fr. Bedford can help me. He's sitting brilliantly profiled by a lamp behind him, the silhouette of his face turned toward a darkened window. Even if he were looking at me I couldn't see his eyes because of the shadow cast be the light in back of him.

Just as I'm about to say something he starts talking again. "St. Thomas Aquinas is a doctor of the Church and the father of something that we call Moderate Realism."

It's then that I notice a long glistening white hair sticking out of the bridge of his nose curving upward like some delicate rhinoceros horn.

"We know that people who have difficulty understanding the logic of Moderate Realism may be experiencing sort of mental aberration. The faculty is very concerned about you." He nods his head toward that darkened window and the white hair trembles.

"The faculty has decided that you should see a therapist to help you with your problem."

I start wondering why Fr. Bedford doesn't see that hair when he looks in the mirror. Or what if he's turning his head sideways like that to show that hair off? There's a long silence. That must mean it's time for me to speak. Thanks to that hair I'm not so afraid. "Father, what if there's quite a few people who don't believe in Moderate Realism, maybe really good, smart people?"

He snaps backwards in his chair for a moment, and then turns his head toward me. I think he's smiling, but I can't tell for sure, because the light behind his head makes his face so dark and vague.

I wonder too if he always speaks to people with that light back there behind him.

Silently he sits up at his desk and passes a note across to me. It crackles as I open it; I see it has the name and phone number of a therapist on it. I'm pretty shaky by this time, but I can still say, "Thank you, Father, I'll call him tomorrow."

"Good."

I'm hazy when I stand up and back away. Before turning around I see his silhouette staring again out the dark window. If he's figuring things out, he's not going to let me in on it.

Back at my seminary I mention the therapist stuff to Johnny. He wonders what a therapist actually does and says he's never tried one but wants me to tell him all the details when I come back. Johnny is really curious.

I mention it to Tim before I go up to my room.

He flashes a sympathetic look at me, like somehow he expected this. Then he turns sideways kind of like Fr. Bedford and says, "You should be glad that you are getting this help now, before it's too late."

His voice sounds urgent and sincere but his caring feels loaded with something much more complex. He's smiling so I know he means to be kind. I remember how I used to really "mean" things back at Mary Valley. I almost laugh for a second because I'm thinking about the word "mean." I didn't know how "mean" I was when I was really "meaning" things. Tim watched me very sympathetically but kind of complacently. I realize that I used to act sympathetically like that too. With renewed kindness, he says he has to go up to his room to study theology. I don't mind him leaving.

Chapter 24

I like the way food is served here; it's called buffet style. A bunch of different kinds of food are put on a table and we actually have some choice about what we want to eat. Sometimes there are even seconds. Life here is a little like a buffet too since there is more free time in which to make choices. I do some of the old things like praying, studying, playing cards, going for walks, but there are knew things too, like writing poetry, drinking coffee at the cafeteria of Catholic University, and getting a tan. Johnny is teaching me about this last activity. He lends me one of his Hawaiian shirts and a pair of his sun glasses, and every Friday as long as the weather holds we go out by the white Madonna and lie in the sun. Sometimes I even take my shirt off; Johnny says the sun will help heal the acne that covers my shoulders and back. During this time we don't even talk. I just feel the sun spreading all over me like warm butter and listen to the sound of traffic zooming by.

There are more choices in how we relate to each

other too. Fr. Murphy says that human affection is good, it's not just an impediment to obedience. This turns out to be pretty promising news for me considering my feelings about Bernie and all the time Johnny and I spend together.

Last Thursday evening Tom Kelly and I were studying in our room. I heard a knock and the door to the room opened. Thursday evening is the time that faculty gets together to talk about us seminarians, to see how we're fitting in. Generally seminarians are a little more subdued on Thursday evenings maybe even on edge.

Now as I answer the door and see Fr. Murphy, I know that he has just stepped out of the faculty meeting.

"Francis, just the man, I wanted to see. I need to talk with you." He looks solemn and nervous.

Fr. Murphy glances at Tom; Tom nods, "I have to go to the library. See you later." Tom sidles past Fr. Murphy. For some reason Fr. Murphy doesn't exactly come into the room but just stands in the doorway. "Francis, doubting is very, very dangerous. Once you start you cannot stop it. Terrible things can happen."

He looks so serious and concerned; I think about what he has said for a minute. "Is doubting always like that Father, no stopping it?"

I must have said something wrong again. His face hardens. He has that look that my dad did when he was getting ready to argue with Dick, something between pleading and threatening. He stares at me like pressure is building up inside him, and if I don't do what he wants he will burst. Maybe to let off a little steam he finally says, "It's not too late for you to stop. You better try." At this point my dad would usual rest his hand on Dick to let him know that everything was still okay in some funny way. Fr. Murphy just stands there a cold look on his face.

I decided that maybe it is my job to let him know that everything is still okay. I thing I can reassure him if I tell him about my seeing the therapist. "I went to my first meeting with the therapist, Father. I'm not exactly sure what he's supposed to do, but I think I'll like having some one to talk to who has a little distance from what's going on around here."

Fr. Murphy shakes his head, "Francis, Francis, Francis," and turning around, leaves.

As I face the empty doorway I think that perhaps Fr. Murphy is really using some sort of secret code. If I can decipher the code I might stand a chance at giving him what he wants.

I do see the therapist regularly, although I'm glad that my parents don't have to be informed. They might worry about me. Every week I get to miss a philosophy class and see this young guy from the Catholic University psychology department who wears turtle necks.

He says he's learning to be a Rogerian therapist. This is about the last thing he says to me because it turns out being a Rogerian therapist means that he just listens to me for an hour saying absolutely nothing while looking embarrassed. Johnny can't make heads or tails out of it either. I do start letting the therapist in on a lot that goes through my mind. I talk about my feelings for Bernie, my night walks with Johnny, and even that little voice inside that helps me out when things get rough. The therapist listens quietly almost like a priest, but instead of giving a penance he only looks very uncomfortable. This may be a code too, but since he doesn't sit in on faculty meetings I start feeling a little affection for him, the way he just sits there.

Chapter 25

Unlike at Mary Valley the outside world seeps in here some. People whisper suspiciously about existentialists and beatniks, but at least there are whispers. Any indication that there is life outside of here has become more important to me. In English class John Austen had us read Joseph Conrad's novel, *Heart of Darkness*. There wasn't even a touch of moderate realism in it. I could tell that John was intrigued by the world of up-side-down values. In class we talked about the end of the story where the narrator doesn't know what's good or bad anymore. Gene laughed in that rolling way of his and said that the guy didn't have his head screwed on properly. Tim started doing that grinding thing again and then said he felt sorry for the narrator. Mario didn't say anything since he's not noticing much lately. Johnny and I were very curious.

I'm not sure through which mysterious channels it came, but I have this idea that my whole class, all five of us, might want to get together and talk about what's going on inside ourselves. I want to give them a chance to talk about insides too. Since Johnny has insides and I do, maybe there's stuff knocking around in them too.

Johnny thinks it's a good idea, of course he's curious about everything. When I talk about it with Mario he lets go of that distant, dignified look and smiles for the first time in weeks. Tim is worried if this meeting would be all right with the faculty; he says that he needs to ask Fr. Murphy's permission. Tim lets me know a few days later that he'll join in; Fr. Murphy must have given his go-ahead. Gene seems reluctant, but when he hears everybody else is going to join in, he decides to go along. That's how it happened.

It's Monday night, one by one we wander down to the recreation room casually as if none of this were planned. Habits of secrecy die slowly here. There's just one light on low, but we can still make out each others faces.

We shuffle around and laugh tightly; I know that I better jump in soon or this whole evening will fall apart.

"Thanks a lot for coming. I'm not completely sure why I'm doing this; but it seems to me that there are all kinds of things going on inside me that I don't talk much about. Maybe you guys have things inside that you have difficulty talking about too. Maybe if we spoke about these things we could get to know each other a little better."

There's a pause. Nobody's laughing; if anything, people look kind of solemn. I glance over to Johnny for reassurance. He nods silently.

"I guess I'll start because it's my idea and there's something going on with me. First, it's been pretty hard here. It seems like we were taught one thing at Mary Valley and another thing here. It's confusing. Lately I've been thinking that maybe neither place is completely right. And then there's this thing about God; I don't know what to believe anymore. Most of the old reasons don't fit.

"There's one last even scarier thing; I'm in love with Bernie Mcquade. I think I've always been attracted to men.

I thought I'd just tell you guys. I guess that's about it for me. I just wanted to tell you guys."

In the dim room quietness takes over and I'm just praying that someone else speaks. Time starts falling through a deep hole and I hear distant rumblings of an approaching accident.

Johnny steps in. "Francis talked about this idea with me a while back. It sounded good. Things here are going fairly smoothly for me. It's not perfect, but neither was Mary Valley. I don't take things too seriously. If it's not too important, I let it pass on by." He chuckles and for a moment the whole room lightens up.

"What is amazing to me is that I'm beginning to look at some real big things differently. Francis and I have had some great old conversations at night, especially about God. Believing isn't simple any more and some of the explanations that we get here seem more like points of view. It's not as dramatic for me as Francis." He pauses.

"Sex...heck, I'm not sure where I'm going with that. Last summer I met a couple of girls I really liked, as people even. There's a girl named Josie who I write to sometimes. I'm not attracted to her, but she's great to talk to. I don't know where any of this is leading, but I'm game to find out. I guess that's about it."

Johnny stops. Just as it is becoming clear that no one else is going to jump in he looks towards Mario and with careful humor and says, "Hey Mario, what's going on with you? You've been quiet as a possum lately."

Mario kind of wrestles in his seat like someone who doesn't want to be disturbed, but is pretty glad still, that somebody nudges him. He sputters like a car in the cold. "You guys, you guys don't want to hear this, you'll just think it's a big joke, just a joke." He laughs in harsh stuttering bursts that are brittle and sharp. "Aw, shit! OK, you asked for it! Last summer, my mother has this friend, last summer this friend invited my family to their swimming pool. We all came. My mother's friend introduces me to her daughter, Bonnie. We talked all afternoon, Bonnie and me, she just had a bathing suite on!"

Gene starts laughing real loudly like he knows what the point is.

"Aw Gene, get outa here, I know what you're

thinking, it's not just that! I really like her. I really do. She says she likes me too. I was never so close to a girl in a bathing suite before. I write her sometimes now…don't laugh at me. It's real serious. I mean it!" He sputters threateningly and stops talking.

There's no laughter now. I think of how I haven't said much to Mario lately and want him to know what he said makes sense to me. "Ya Mario, feelings are really confusing."

Mario laughs but softer.

Johnny echoes, "You can say that again."

Tim jumps in quickly, like if he doesn't do it now, he never will and something in him all tangled up really wants to break out. "I don't know how much I should say. I talked to Fr. Murphy and he said this meeting might be all right; I really like it here. All the priests are so nice. They treat me like I'm important. I would never want to do anything that would get them upset; I really like it here."

There's a long pause, but you can tell he's not done because he starts drilling his finger into his nose like he's worried about something. He looks up and out with an expression on his face I've never seen before, smiling like he just wants to say hello or something simple like that. "I don't know about being attracted to men. Fr. Murphy says you can love men without being `that way.' I don't know." He gets all tight again, like he is frightened to see where he is and wants to forget about what he said.

I say, "Ya Tim," and try to get his attention by

nodding. Gene starts laughing again and almost on signal Tim starts laughing too as if everything he said before was a mistake. Before my eyes whatever Tim was trying to say gets erased.

Gene holds on to the center stage. "I don't know what the big hairy deal is. We talk or we don't talk. Things are great around here. Fr. Murphy says I have what it takes. Whether I like guys, that's my business. Father says it's okay that I get my warm fuzzies wherever I can get them as long as things don't get out of hand. When Tony gets here next year I'll really be set. It's my business and I'm doing just fine. If anybody's having problems here it's their own fault." He starts laughing. I try to laugh with him but something pulls tight inside.

What he says sounds complicated and scary to me but still he's talking about it, so it's important. I just don't have words; I get this way a lot around Gene lately.

Suddenly I now it's all over; this is about as far as we can go. We throw uncomfortable but relieved glances at each other. Someone says, "We have to do this again." It's enough for me; I can see other people have insides too.

Things go on pretty ordinarily after this, but for me life is a little less complicated. One last event happens a few weeks later that may be connected to our meeting.

Mario walks into my room at about 8:30 PM looking so dignified that he's frozen. He sits down.

I say, "Hi, Mario" and finish what I'm writing. It almost seems like he just wants to sit there rigidly. I look up in a minute and want to say something soft but feel like the least motion on my part might shatter him into pieces. Finally he slumps down and looks like the little scared boy that I knew those first years at Mary Valley.

"Francis something really strange happened. I don't know what…I can't tell you what…one of our classmates came in…I can't tell you who…I had my shirt off…into my room…he sat right next to me. I can't tell you who it is…he started saying he loved me and kept feeling up my chest for a real long time… didn't know what to do…he kept touching me all over my chest, again and again…kept touching…"

I don't know what to do except to feel sad and not touch him.

Then he starts looking real dignified again and I know that I better say something fast. "Mario, that guy shouldn't have done that. I don't think love is what he was doing. I'm so sorry that happened to you. You're my friend." And then I don't have anymore words so we just sit there for a while.

Right before Mario becomes completely dignified again he says like in explanation, "I can't tell you who it was, he made me promise." After that I notice that Mario doesn't talk much to anybody anymore; just a little to Johnny and me.

After the thing with Mario it seems to me that the more out in the open things are the better. Who ever did that to Mario, had lots of things bouncing around trapped inside, so much so that he hurt Mario badly instead of loving him.

It's really a bind with some things; you get punished if you let them out, but if you don't, they get all twisted and you hurt someone else and still maybe get punished. About all I know how to do is just begin letting things sort out, just around the edges where they're already unraveling.

Chapter 26

Life edges into spring here. I love spring; things seem more possible. Lately on Sunday afternoons, some of us jump into a pick up truck and head over to other seminaries to play basketball. This whole Washington area is scattered with seminaries of different religious orders. I go because in the last few years I've actually grown into the habit of playing sports. I am incredibly clumsy. Of course it helps that Bernie's usually there.

The truck from the major seminary stops by and Johnny, Mario, and me jump onto the open back and join the other guys. The air is gray and damp but warm smelling of the sweet rot of early spring. When the truck gets to the other seminary clear on the other side of town, Johnny and I hang back talking about God. Suddenly remembering the basketball game we rush into the locker room pushing the door open. In a flash of lightening, I see Bernie spot lit facing me naked surrounded by the other guys who are also changing into gym clothes. The whole scene is frozen like a photograph except for Bernie's eyes that move to glance out at me. Our eyes make contact and I want to throw up. The thunder of an accident rolls in. In all my years in the seminary I have never seen a man's body naked from the front. I feel queasy and don't ever want to see Bernie again. Words don't fit here because it was a picture-feeling, but I see skinny, green legs splaying out from Bernie's slimy, frog hips. Then the thunder echoes away too. I hear Bernie's voice saying, "So there you guys are, I thought we lost you," and the flashing storm is over; we are all just getting ready for the game; I'm in love with him again.

Later that afternoon, once in a while watching Bernie leap on the court with all his power and grace I see a frog, like a being intruding from another world branded somewhere deep inside me. Having been raised a Catholic with all those amazing and miraculous stories I can take this in and even remember some of it.

By the time the game's over and we're showered and changed, it's a raw chilly evening. We pile into the open back of the truck again. The older seminarians take positions sheltered against the cab of the truck, protected from the blasts of wind. A moment of embarrassment touches everybody; what's to happen to the younger guys, Johnny, Mario, and me sitting towards the back and exposed to the rushing cold? It's funny we've been taught to be nice or good but seldom to care about each other. Bernie breaks the silence, "Francis, you can come over here."

I can hardly register the sound of his voice, not just because it's his voice but the idea of him wanting to take care of me seems impossible. I just look at Bernie like I'm paralyzed. He gently, with a little pirate smile, gestures me to lean up against him, sheltered. His back is against the cab and he spreads his legs and arms open for me. What do you do when the universe opens and beckons you into its embrace, but you can't quite feel it? I've spent years being careful, separating before things could be taken away from me. I can't stop being separate and kind of anxious and numb at the same. Tightly strung I sit between Bernie's legs but can't lean back for fear my head and neck will rest against his groin. The frog thing flashes and thunders for a moment. It's not a question of sin anymore, life isn't that simple now. I'm also not one hundred per cent sure that Bernie really wants me to rest against that part of his body. Partly I feel an accident brewing but mostly my fear has no name. Very nonchalantly he places his hands over his abdomen and props my head up so that I'm not forced to step through that fear with no name. Our bodies meet on a shore of confusion and kindness.

The truck starts moving. Opening my eyes I see the night above me filled with stars rushing by like those Christmas lights I saw from the bus so long ago. Bernie's hand steadies my head; I feel the rise and fall of his breaths lulling me. His sad, ironic laughter runs through me.

I know that wonder is just on the other side of

my anxiety only a second or two away. That second or two wrenches my stomach with numb regret. And then I start thinking how my time with Bernie will be over too soon; he is going to spend the next two year in Cleveland, teaching at a Catholic school there. I can feel the tearing. My silent self whispers that it's best not to feel this too strongly. Something deep inside complies. I close my eyes and hide in the grey rocking of his breath.

The brakes of the truck squeal to a stop, my eyes still closed, I'm loosened from his arms by the truck's sudden halt. Gently I bounce back slightly against Bernie's hand and forbidden groin. I open my eyes and get up like someone walking into some inevitable fate.

"Thanks Bernie."

"Any time Francis."

We're in front of my seminary; I jump off the back of the truck with Johnny and Mario. Landing on the ground my feet don't move, like my body is stuck in a dream. I watch myself looking through this long tunnel of night into which that truck with Bernie in it disappears. Then Johnny says, "Are you all right Francis?"

And now there's only one of me again and I'm just standing there in the dark. I say, "Sure." We walk back together, but I don't have any words for this; it's not spy stuff; I just don't have any words even for Johnny. I walk back into our building of lights and card games and Masses. I leave something out there in the dark, looking into the distance.

Chapter 27

Maybe that's why I like to walk in the night; I'm looking for something. One night Johnny and I start walking; we have to sneak out to do this. Of course I don't want to be caught by the priests, but there is no inner sense of badness about my decision. We sneak out the door in back, careful to leave it unlocked. We start walking. In the far distance we see the glow of downtown Washington. We can see the lit up capital dome floating like a vision way far away. It calls to us.

Johnny's quieter than usual like something is on his mind. Walking such a far distance gives us plenty of time to get at things. Finally he starts like he's midway in his thinking, and he knows I'll catch up. "Francis, maybe it's not really figuring out that's so important." He pauses to let that sink in. "Do you remember when we used to play baseball at Mary Hill?"

"Ya, I do; when we came to Washington I promised myself I'd never do that again."

"You'd stand out there in right field. Even though you looked real earnest, I could tell that you were praying that no one would hit the ball out there. The pitcher threw the ball, there was a sharp cracking sound, and the ball was suddenly arching into right field. At first you followed the ball with your head and started running towards the vicinity of where it was coming, and then you froze with your glove pointing in the general direction of the batter. I worried because I could tell that you had stopped looking at the ball; I though you might get hit on the head or something. You put yourself in the right position but wouldn't look at what was coming at you. You missed the ball but you could have been hurt to."

I listen reassured by the rhythm of our steps together. "I suppose I can't watch something that's coming at me that way. I hear the `crack' and I know it's headed at me fast and vicious. I know I should catch it, but kind of automatically I go somewhere else. From somewhere else I keep trying to figure out what to do."

He glances sideways at me. "I saw you do that with your ideas about God too. I watched you experience new stuff that none of us were thinking about. You heard that bat `crack' sending something in your direction; you even followed it for a while but then you closed your eyes, and the priests they're just ordinary people, and they start to think you're crazy."

I just let the words sink in. It's easy to take the words in without closing my eyes because I know

Johnny likes me. Finally my thoughts come together. "Johnny, I grew up with this story about God. I didn't think much about it because most of the time I knew who I was in the story and what I should do. Then the story started to evaporate, but by this time my whole life was built on the story and now I'm evaporating too, except for those few moments where I feel excited about learning something new. But mostly I'm left just being alone knowing that terrible stuff is going to happen to me. The priests are just the start. I know it and I keep trying harder to stop that thing coming at me. My head just turns away. I can't look at what's coming at me no matter what. All I can do is pretend I want to see, so nobody punishes me and speeds up that thing headed in my direction."

The lit up dome of the capitol is getting closer now like some sort of dream. Johnny listens carefully and then starts warming up to talk. "I don't know why, but I've always wanted to look at the ball especially if it's coming at me. Doesn't mean I always catch it, but I'm more likcly too and less likely to get beaned. I also know I don't feel things as strongly as you do, that's one of the reasons I like you; you keep me on my toes." He smiles at me.

"You see Johnny I keep having this dream where I'm a spy and all I can do is run through these empty buildings waiting to be caught by someone I never see. I wake up, and being attracted to men and all I know there's not much of a life waiting out there for me, just this empty place where seminarians disappear.

But there's been times in this last year when I stopped running so much and started to look out; I felt a kind of breeze, like it wasn't just me thinking, but I was actually there, really there. Then those stories about a threatening God that the priests tell seem like their way of closing their eyes because something is racing towards them. They try to stop me looking out because they're afraid that they might have to look too."

Johnny nods thoughtfully as we walk along. "Those beliefs about God, even good old Thomas Aquinas' ideas still reassure me most times, but I'll keep listening to you and enjoying our figuring out. I know it's not crazy, just real, real intense."

We finally reach the capitol; all the streets are dark empty and haunted but with Johnny it feels pretty fine. We catch a bus back at 2AM. The driver scolds us for walking late at night in downtown Washington. He makes us promise not to do it ever again. This feels good to me; his advice isn't complicated like the priests'.

At about this time I start making another friend this time at the major seminary, almost by accident. It happens during one of those times I go over there hoping Bernie will notice me. I'm pretty preoccupied on the inside but probably look lost on the outside. A deep voice shakes me.

"Hi, I'm Don."

This huge hand covered with black hair enters my field of vision and opens like a big flower. Still trying to keep my mind's eye on Bernie I glance up and see an even bigger face with a smile on it that shifts between bewilderment and kindness. Tender eyes show through the black stubble that covers his face.

"Nice to meet you, my name's Francis...hi."

If this were Bernie, he'd start marking his territory around me, but Don holds his distance. "Yes I know. Some of the guys here say you're right out of the Middle Ages and others say that you're dangerously close to being an existentialist. I thought I might want to get to know someone with so much latitude."

Maybe it's that bewildered look on his face or just the way he stands there ordinary but interested, I let go of Bernie and decide to start figuring out things with Don. "I don't know if it's latitude or confusion, but I sure can't pin things down anymore. It seems to make the priests even more nervous than I am about it all."

"Well you're not alone in the wondering department. I'm putting pieces together for myself. If you ever need someone to talk to, stop up and see me."

Then we both get embarrassed at the same time and smile; we remember other things we have to do. Now when we run into each other we talk, nothing real deep yet, but we are warming up.

Chapter 28

One morning at the very beginning of April, I wake up excited like if I don't get up right away I'll miss something. I look out the window. All March the weather had been unpredictable; sometimes chilly, sometimes mild. Last night a warm steady spring finally settled in, green flooding everything, soft and determined. In all that pulsing of spring my fears seem more like a memory. I may even be able to handle one of the dilemma's facing me.

Bernie is going away next year to teach for a while at one of our order's high schools in Chicago. Sometimes major seminarians do this like a kind of time out before ordination to the priesthood. Mostly for me this means another goodbye to Bernie. When he's not around, some part of my life disappears, and I go dormant until he's back. I'm still at a loss for words around him so we don't really figure things out together, but there's a way he snaps me into a bigger world of clumsy possibility. Besides I'm used to his periodic tenderness when he shares his magic with me.

I'm going to tell Bernie that I love him. It seems real natural. I want him to know because that's the way I feel, the love I mean. He'll still be going away for a while, but maybe if he knows about my feelings then that bigger world that he snaps me into will be more part of my life not just this little surprise that comes from him. I suppose Gene would say I want something even more than that and then would laugh. But I won't think about anything more than just talking.

This kind of talking isn't without precedent at this seminary. Sex is out of the question, but there is a certain tolerance even respect for feeling some emotions. Fr. Murphy with all his confusing drama, leaves this as a legacy. In some ways though, he treats emotions the way that he treats that fish of his. You can feel what you like as long as it is contained in that little glassed in space, finally a very small place. If those feelings ever were to break out they would be all wild and desperate gasping for air. Either Tim or Gene broke out of a fragile restraint that night when one of them went into Mario's room and kept touching his chest while he sat frozen scared. I'm still all in glass around Bernie, but if I indicate to him what's going on with me maybe I won't hurt him and even better I'll make more room for myself.

After going through these thoughts I walk over to the major seminary on this spring evening so impossibly beautiful that hope seems real. The soft evening light floods through the door of the recreation room there, displacing the usual dark, smoky staleness that reminds me of the priests' recreation room at Mary Hill. Bernie's here; I can tell without looking… there he is…he's alone…this is my chance. I scuttle across the room.

"Bernie would you like to go for a walk with me?" I'm startled by the sound of my own voice.

He looks surprised for a second, caught off guard. He pauses as if trying to get this experience of someone else initiating an action into better focus. Then, "Sure Francis, let's go."

We step out into the tender evening. Being in charge helps me get a little closer to the feeling of how wonderful it is to have him by my side. I know I have time; he won't go away until I finish. I feel inside that he cares for me in some kind way like in the back of the truck a month ago.

I decide to stay in the lead. "You see Bernie, there's something I want to tell you. I know you're going away next year…I want to tell you before you go."

"Sure, I'm listening." He touches me on the shoulder just for a moment, but long enough so I know he means what he says.

I hear the sounds of our feet brushing against the pavement; it's not so much that I'm afraid, but this is something I've never done before. I charge myself up by walking and just when silence builds up so much pressure that I'm ready to burst I leap over the edge of my imagination. "I've known you for five years now. During all that time you treated me kindly; I just want to say that I love you." I sail downwards in the quiet of the evening.

There is a moment in which only the sound of our feet brushing against the road echoes through the evening like a sacrament.

Then Bernie's voice rings like bells at evening benediction, startling and solemn all at the same time. He says my name, "Francis." He pauses long enough so that I know he's caught me. "Thanks for telling me. I thought something was up." He flashes his pirate smile again, except this time he finishes it off softly. "People here talk about love, but use it in funny ways." He's real serious now, figuring something out as we walk. "I think St. Paul's right in the part of his letter to the Corinthians, something about, if I speak with the tongues of angels and do not have love I'm like clanging symbols. Love is patient and kind, bearing and forgiving all things. Francis, do you understand any of this?"

He sounds like me when I'm trying to talk about God, hopeful but not counting on people understanding. I know that I don't understand everything that he is saying, but something about it rings true; I want to hear more. I pause a minute and nod so he knows for sure I'm listening. "Ya Bernie, I think I do, at least enough for a start." I can tell he is happy about someone listening to him carefully.

He pauses, studying me kindly, "There's something...something about love...more than just getting what you want." He's struggling to put pieces together.

Very gently I nod at him.

"Love has something to do with service, actually caring about what happens to another person."

For an instant I see Bernie as another person…real and sometimes maybe even confused. "I don't know much about service. Mostly I feel too afraid. But it helps me to hear you talk about it. It's a possibility now even for me."

He looks at me very intently. "You're tough as nails Francis." He smiles with something like admiration.

I smile back, not shyly. "I know."

He looks reassured, but kind of lonely. I wonder what price he pays carrying so many of our dreams.

Then without interrupting the rhythm of our pace, we talk about more ordinary things; easing down from gold to grey to black with the night.

The black isn't the color of hopelessness. It's the color of diving in all alone not knowing for sure what's going to happen. I feel happy being caught and restless at the same time. I talked with Bernie; he listened. But this really isn't a happy ending in which I can dissolve. It's just one leap early in the beginning of some trip on which he can't go with me. You see, it's not just Bernie going away but me too, not because I want to go away, but because something seems to call me over and over again. No matter how close I get to somebody there's always a going away at night.

"Bernie," I touch his shoulder, "Thanks a lot. Can I come up and see you before you go?"

"Sure kid."

It's over; I leave him sitting on a bench in the dark not forlorn or anything, just sitting looking out into the future.

I go back and talk about it a little with Johnny. He thinks it went pretty well. I can't explain even to him that there's something sad about it all. I'm in this new place; not heaven or hell. There are things to do. It's not a vacation to look forward to, but something that starts now and starts now for me. I'm still saying goodbye to Bernie in the dark.

Last day of school I stop at the major seminary to say good bye to Bernie. He's surrounded by five or six guys: a natural center. I hear his voice weaving in and out of the talking. Something slips into my thinking that is so new, it doesn't have a name yet. I'm disturbed that he's busy with everybody else and that everybody else is busy with him. I fell betrayed and angry; I want to punish somebody, maybe Bernie.

I wonder about this. What's different? This is how Bernie has been ever since I've known him. I love him; why do I want to hurt him? There was a time just hearing his name was enough. Thinking about that evening on which I told him I love him, I can almost see that peculiar sadness on his face. I even remember that thing that he said about love bearing all and forgiving all like it's not some sort of a contract written on paper for which non-compliance should be punished.

I have to catch my bus soon. I can't step into that magic circle to wait for his attention. I also know that I don't hate him; I love him. I walk away hearing the voices in the distance fade. Bernie's is the last voice that I hear.

Chapter 29

Back in St. Paul I still go to Mass on Sundays. I even go to confession a couple of times, but I'm not so sure anymore what makes things a sin or why anybody should be punished. After all those years of being afraid of going to hell, that fear begins evaporating. I wish I could say that makes me happy, but in its place I start making out the edges of another fear that's both old and new; there's no heaven to get away from being afraid. I can't escape the crushing story that I'm in this big dead mechanical universe. This machine doesn't even need monsters. It just grinds people up while they're alive just like with Chris and now with me. Maybe all the figuring out is just a distraction from the inevitable.

I can tell that my parents are aware that something is different with me. They seem to sense that I'm not quite so sure of myself. No one actually questions me; I've been careful to insulate them from my confusion. Like I said before, they don't even know about the therapist. The wonderful things about last year would even be harder to talk about; the words describing that stuff wouldn't quite make sense here. Besides the seminary is a hot house; those tender, exotic things I'm learning would just shrivel up in the outside.

There's trouble back here too; not just the ordinary amount that people eventually laugh about. Dick is in the army in Vietnam. My parents worry; Dick has a way of inviting disaster.

Almost like life doesn't happen fast enough for him, so he starts taking crazy risks just to keep things hopping.

Chris is in the Navy safe from physical harm, but on his last visit home he seemed like he had leapt off of some edge beyond his imagination too, but he was left alone in some wild, trapped way all turned inward. He's started writing strange letters to my parents that sound like nightmares. I was the predictable one of their three sons, and now they know there's something wrong with me too.

Some nights I watch my dad step away from the television set and sit out on the front stoop, just staring out into the evening. Is he worrying about Dick or Chris? I don't want him to worry about me, so I don't join him on the stoop. Sometimes though when he comes in he has a soft almost relaxed look on his face. He comes up to me and says things like, "Francis, I'm real proud of you son."

I can tell my mother misses all the activity in the house. There's nothing more that she can do to shore things up. After all the struggle, she's left with just waiting. She has always had a harder time letting things happen, just like me.

Some nights, I pretend to be really interested in the late movie. My dad says, "Good night, Francis," and goes over to my mom who's trying to keep busy doing at least two things at the same time and says, "Joannie, why don't you come to bed with me now?"

Not that it's brilliant dialogue or anything, but after my mom kisses me good night, she follows him into the bedroom and closes the door. I hear her laugh in that soft way that girls do sometimes.

This time they both come with me to the bus station. Together we walk into that busy place where people sit awhile before they go away; each of us worried about the other. We sit on those hard plastic chairs waiting in suspense until that absolutely confident voice on the loud speaker calls out my bus. We all stand there stuck for a few seconds with no words to cover ourselves. Then just when I have to rush away, dad says, "Son, are you all right?" I just have time to reassure him, "I'm fine dad." He hugs me anyway, like a coded message, just in case things aren't so fine. Mom hugs me too; I think of all those other departures when I left her holding the fort. How do I let her know that my future is crumbling?

I walk seriously to the bus, but before I enter it again I turn and flash a pirate smile as I disappear into my last year in the seminary.

Chapter 30

I start out my year in Washington by writing two letters. The first one, like collecting a reward, is to Bernie. I write him all the usual stuff about school coming along fine and the weather. The second letter is more complicated because it's to my brother Chris and it has to do with remembering things. When I was eight and he was ten, Chris started questioning and wondering about things. I'm not sure why, but life was pretty desperate back then. I suppose I was so used to life feeling that way that I didn't even have a name for it. It's funny when things are so big, you can't see them from the outside; you're just part of them. To me it seemed that my family carried this kind of doom around that was as familiar as the color of our eyes, something beyond comment because it was just us. Since separating from them five years ago, it's like I've been trying to get far enough away from that disaster so I wouldn't get pulled down too. Getting separate from them gave me a little space to maneuver. I started going away from them for almost as long as I can remember.

All this while Chris was asking big questions so big they threw everyone off balance; like why should people be punished by God when they only made a mistake, or with the world being so messed up why is everybody so sure there is a God or that he's a good God?

Even back then Chris started writing. I don't remember much except a story about a girl whose insides were like those rainbows that surprise you after a storm. When she talked about those colors people became angry because they didn't want to be reminded of the storm. They tore at her face leaving her silent with tattered dull eyes. Even now when I get sad I think about that girl's raggedy eyes.

Back then I didn't argue with Chris, I just tried to urgently explain that if he doubted the things we all believed in, our lives would collapse. Back then I thought I could show Chris the ropes; I didn't realize he was already hanging from them. He kept reminding me about things I didn't want to look at; I couldn't just listen to him, like Johnny. Chris was so young, he couldn't even check adult books out of the library.

I don't know why some people fall through to places where other people can't hear them. One day I think Chris decided that no one was going to ever understand him and finally he let go, kind of like when you're walking in a rainstorm that'll never end, getting wetter and wetter, worrying about it all the time. When suddenly you hear your feet making sloshing sounds inside your shoes and you finally give up, knowing that it doesn't matter any more. The rain keeps coming.

This letter is the first time I say I'm sorry not out of fear, but just because I'm sorry for not being there when he was coming alive in a new way.

I get a response from Chris very quickly. It's the last time anyone in my family would hear from him for many years, and then he'd be at a psychiatric hospital after he threw a brick through a church window. A policeman said that he just stood there motionless next to the gaping, ragged hole of broken rainbow colored glass.

His words in this last letter was kind and dignified.

Dear Francis,

Thanks for your letter. I'm sorry that things are particularly hard for you right now.

You don't need to apologize, you see, I can hardly remember anything that happened back then. But thanks anyway.

Your Bother,
Chris

Just like Chris I start to write now, too. It's a life line. My whole life is like one of those foreground-background puzzles. First you just see two dark silhouetted faces looking at each other. For the life of you, you can't see anything else. Then all of a sudden as if by accident you glance at it and see a white chalice against a dark background. It was always there, you just couldn't see it. It takes a little practice to first see one image and then the other. I am introduced to a new self, not just inside and not just outside, but someone who can switch back and forth.

Johnny, Mario, Tim, and Gene all come back for our sixth year. Johnny is as curious as ever. Mario bristles with the defiance. Tim is like a fish in a bowl. Gene has his long awaited friend Tony as his roommate. Some of the pressure is loosened for me because I have a new room mate too, Darryl Wozniack. He seems really nervous but tries to be friendly. He doesn't watch me the way Tom Kelly did. Darryl is even skinnier than I am and attended another seminary leaving under circumstances which he won't talk about.

Now, information disseminates here in mysterious ways and the word is out that the priests here are giving Darryl one last chance; almost immediately a circle of silence forms around him. It's like desperation has a smell that drives other people away. A bunch of guys are talking, Darryl walks in the room, everyone else starts getting restless, and before you can say Ave Maria, Darryl is standing alone. Yet I bet if you asked any of these guys what happened they'd say that they suddenly thought of something they needed to do. They might even be sincerely upset that someone was questioning their motives; it's important to be kind here.

I think Darryl is attracted to men too. This isn't unusual around here, but he doesn't seem to have a knack for bending his behavior into an acceptable shape. He's not satisfied with just feeling in love like me, and he doesn't know how to sneak in what Gene calls "his warm fuzzies" either; Darryl looks hungry. That kind of hungry frightens me.

He doesn't get a lot of information about how to behave because people instinctually avoid him. Gene doesn't miss much, I have to hand it to him; he notices things. He periodically laughs and mentions to everyone how much Darryl and I look and act alike; I'm clearly not on the inside of this joke.

I wish I was braver; I find myself being friendly to Darryl, but kind of distant. At moments I feel like he is my future. Just as Bernie carries so many of our hopes; Darryl carries so many of our fears. He looks lonely and sexual. I do show him around here, but he's already so nervous and with that circle of silence around him I can tell he doesn't stand much of a chance here. We talk in a friendly way and go for walks sometimes and but still there's some way I keep him at arms' length.

One evening I'm playing pinochle with Johnny, Tim, and Gene like life here could go on forever. Darryl rushes in, his long black cassock unable to hide some wild urgency.

"Francis I really need to talk with you." He looks me straight in the eyes pleading.

I don't want to step out of this moment of shelter,

but as Gene and Tim exchange glances I know that I have nothing to loose. Maybe even a little I remember something about Chris and the way I said I was sorry. "Ah, sure Darryl," and I step into the storm. "Let's go for a walk."

As we leave the rec room, I try to blot out of my mind's eye Gene's laughing face and the ripple of laughter that reverberates from it. When Darryl and I get outside I notice that he's shaking.

"I got a letter today from the man I was having sex with last summer. I don't know how he found out where I am. I keep reading the letter over and over again and I remember how it was last summer. I want sex so badly, I don't know what to do!"

I just kind of keep walking, acting like he told me something pretty ordinary instead of amazingly frightening. "That sounds really difficult Darryl." I touch his shoulder slightly just to let him know I am here.

It's like having someone to talk with, allows him to let go a little further; he really starts shaking now. "Sometimes I need sex so badly, I don't know what to do. I want to stand out on the road and try to get someone to pick me up."

By this time I'm glad it's evening, because I don't know what to say and I don't even want to think about it. I just know I'm supposed to be here. Darryl keeps talking not so much about ideas but feelings whistling out of a pressure cooker.

I know I need to say things that'll let him know

I'm listening, but I still need to warn him against doing something dangerous. Finally I remember that bus driver from last year, how he cautioned Johnnie and me not to walk the streets of Downtown Washington at night; in a way that felt good. I stop the rhythm of our pace and stand looking directly at Darryl's shadowy face. "I don't know how this all fits in, but I don't think being with men in a sexual way is bad. I want it too, although it still scares me. I do know that I don't want you to hurt yourself and maybe that might happen if you got picked up on the road tonight. I want you to promise me that you won't do that."

He nods reluctantly.

We start walking quietly and I notice how the moon has a big floppy halo around it. I point it out to Darryl. Quite suddenly whatever was happening to him is over. His face relaxes a little, "I promise."

We walk around a few minutes talking about simpler stuff before we go back in.

Within a few weeks Darryl is asked to leave. He asks me to go on one last walk. I hesitate and then say yes. He is being cast out from the shelter of the seminary; I can recognize the silent circle of judgment around him. He asks me to visit him in Chicago on my bus trip this summer to my family in Minnesota; he even hands me a piece of paper with his name and phone number on it. I nod reluctantly and say goodbye.

At least I say goodbye.

A week after he leaves, I decide to take Don, that

big guy from the major seminary, up on his standing invitation. As I walk up to his room I'm thinking how easy it is to come up to see him. This is a sure sign I'm not in love with him. It just feels nice to be going up to see an older, kind man; especially since the priests here act so strained and distant. I knock on the door; a deep voice inside says, "Come in." I walk in pretty casually and then my world splits open to reveal Don lying in bed, naked except for a small towel over his groin; a vision of a large, strong, hairy man lying in front of me. I start backing out of the door as if it's someone else's dream.

He notices my embarrassment, looks bewildered for a moment, notices his situation and then gets embarrassed too. But like I said before, Don is gentle. He laughs apologetically, "It's all right Francis; you can come in. We just had some wine downstairs and everything is spinning. How are you?" He takes up the conversation like we just met in the rec room instead of in his bedroom while he's almost naked.

When I hear he wants me to stay I realize that it's real, not just a dream. I can stay and talk with him while he squirms under that little towel. I'm past the stage in my own life where I worry about sin a lot, but I don't want to do anything too drastic around here; even looking at a naked man direct on seems drastic. As long as I look at his eyes and leave the hairy maleness to kind of swim in my peripheral vision, I'm okay. It helps that he keeps smiling kindly as he tries to collect the pieces of his dignity. "Ah, I'm pretty good, Don. You said that thing about coming up to see you if I want to talk…decided to take you up on that."

"Come and sit down, don't mind me, I'm glad you're here." In spite of his being pretty close to his ordination to the priesthood he still doesn't seem to protect secrets relentlessly. I follow his lead and talk casually as if we are in the middle of figuring things out. "It's funny Don, the harder I try to not question things the more doubts flood in. What's hard is not having the words to describe them, especially to the priests."

Don looks at me real seriously like he's hardly bewildered by finding himself looking up at me from his bed. "Yeah, the seminary is a difficult place for learning new things." He laughs, in spite of his best efforts the tipsiness occasionally breaks through. Between my looking only at his eyes and both of us talking about God, we do all right for ten minutes.

Don and I see each other about once a week now. I talk about God, the seminary, my love for Bernie; I even tell Don, that I'm attracted to him.

He tells me things to. One day after I tell him some of the things that happened to me as a kid… the thing with Bud, he's silent for a few minutes and then starts up talking like words can be difficult for him, too.

"I've never told anybody about this, Francis. Until you mentioned what happened to you I had forgotten all about it. I was about eleven, in sixth grade, but already I was getting real big. Inside my body was changing real fast. I'd get hardons half the day. I hated it because some days I couldn't even get up from my desk without everybody noticing. Most of the other boys weren't having that dilemma yet, and they thought that it was the funniest thing in the whole world. One day a bunch of us were messing around in the locker room, snapping towels and things like that, and I got an erection. I tried to hide it, but it just wouldn't go down. The other guys noticed. They started wrestling with me laughing and saying, 'Don's got a boner! Don's got a boner!' While a few guys held me down, a couple more of them masturbated me. I fought as hard as I could and then my cock just exploded...I didn't want to cum...I didn't!"

He kind of shudders and becomes real quiet. I just listen and feel sad about what was torn from him. "I'm real sorry that happened to you Don. Thanks for telling me."

Then it's like he's gathering all the pieces of his dignity together again and says, "I think homosexuality is just a stage you go through." He looks to me for reassurance.

The way things are going for me, I don't have much to give him.

We go swimming together sometimes in a pool at Catholic University. My erect cock stretches the front of my swim suite when we horse around. We both laugh easily and continue to become friends.

Chapter 31

ut things don't go so smoothly as far as Bernie is
concerned. At the beginning of the year I wrote
him a letter. One week, two weeks, four weeks, two
months…no answer. I get crazy about it and start
feeling all kinds of desperate and suspicious things,
like he's just making fun of me. One night I make
the leap and write him another letter.

"Dear Bernie,

I'm writing you again. I don't know why you
haven't written to me. I've waited two months and I
haven't heard from you.

I'm wondering if everything we talked about last
spring is a joke for you. Are you just making fun of
me? Please write me.

Sincerely,
Francis

Both Johnny and Don suggest that I hold on to
the letter for a couple of days before I send it. I send it

right away. Almost immediately I feel shocked about what I've done. Six years ago I just wanted Bernie to remember my name, and now I get angry because he doesn't write me a letter. It's like being angry at God. It's not like with Johnny or Don.

I must look pretty wild and distracted to the faculty. They've stopped dropping ominous hints and don't even ask me questions in class anymore. I'd like to explain to them what's going on, but I'm in this place that I barely understand myself. When I do reach out to them with pretty simple stuff, they treat me like there is something wrong with me. Talking with Johnny and Don helps me see that what I'm feeling is human, but still I'm closer to some kind of panic. It's like I'm climbing higher and higher; at first I feel exhilarated seeing the tops of things. But then I realize that this long pole I'm on is starting to wobble and dip. I'm miles above everybody else and I'm wobbling uncontrollable into bigger and bigger circles. Everything spins around me. I rush through the air waiting for the final dip that breaks off my perch and sends me plummeting down.

The priests and most of the other seminarians look at me in this special way as if they're in on some sort of secret about me, but they're too kind to talk about it in front of me. Or maybe I am really going crazy. I'm still seeing the therapist, but just reporting my life to a silent embarrassed looking listener isn't enough to stop the wild dipping. I try to look more animated in class, but I still end out saying the wrong things.

It's a little like a movie I saw along time ago where this guy keeps trying to talk with people because he can't get it through his head that he has already died in an accident.

As an attempt to get through to people I set up another one of those meetings with my classmates. Johnny is all for it. Mario says he really doesn't care one way or the other, but he'll show up. Tim is reluctant until Gene decides that they'll come.

From the start of the evening everything is different from last time. Things start out late and loud. I'm the first one down; even Johnny is a few minutes late. Tim comes down nervous because he's missing out on time to study for a philosophy quiz. Mario drops in and sits in a far corner as if he's not here. Finally Gene barges in, "Lets get this show on the road." And off we go at a frantic pace.

Without waiting, Mario starts talking real defiantly like he's got to prove something. "I'm writing Bonnie two times a week now. This summer we kissed; and it felt good. You guys don't know what you're missing. I'm starting to hate it here…as if the priests know anything. They try to make me go to Mass everyday. My spiritual director asked me if I'm going to go to the novitiate next year, and I told him I'll think about it."

Tim slips in. "Mario, we're supposed to obey the rules. We have to."

"Tim, get out of my face. You don't know anything either!"

Gene chimes in,"You're going to get in trouble Mario, you just wait and see."

"Get out of my face!"

Tim starts talking determinedly as if he is righting some dangerous situation. "Some of you guys don't realize how much the faculty cares about us. Just the other day Fr. Murphy said how much they all like me. They know what's right for us and we should obey them."

"I can hardly wait to go to the novitiate next year. Some of you guys better watch out. The faculty knows what goes on here." Then he stops very quickly like he's said too much and nervously glances at Gene for reassurance. The whole evening is racing away, and I decide I better jump in. "Things still feel pretty funny to me. When I ask questions the priests become upset, when I just sit back and listen they say I look spaced out. I don't know what to do. What makes things even harder is that I feel real crazy about not having heard from Bernie. I wrote him this letter..."

Gene starts laughing, "I'm sure glad my honey likes me!"

I can't even pretend to laugh and start forgetting about what else I might want to talk about. "Oh, I guess that's about it. I suppose everything is all right."

Gene's on a roll now. "What's the big hairy deal? My honey is here now. We can role around anytime as long as we don't go too far. It's all real simple. Fr. Murphy says that it's just getting warm fuzzies and I don't have to be worried about being one way or another. He says I'll love the novitiate." And then Gene stops real quickly and looks at me like he's let some cat out of the bag.

The pace finally slows, not that people ever looked ready to talk to each other. Mario is turned sideways like he's just getting ready to escape. Tim is sitting all inward and still like he's in church and doesn't want to be distracted. Gene is creaking in his chair every few moments dramatically changing position.

Johnny starts. "My spiritual director brought up the novitiate to me too. I suppose I'll try it and see what happens." He pauses for a second too. He turns to me like he is trying to prepare me for something. "Francis, if I were going to be stuck on a deserted island with only one person I'd pick you."

I feel glad and maybe a little embarrassed. I can't quite make the connection between him wanting to go to the novitiate and letting me know he likes me. Aren't we all going there if we want? Still I'm glad for what he says because it means that what I'm going through is intelligible and maybe even likable.

Then we all sit for a moment, stuck, like there's no where else to go and nothing more to say. After a few uncomfortable moments everyone disappears into their own dreams. Wobbling and dipping, I'm the last to leave.

A week later I hear that Bernie is coming back to visit Washington for the weekend. I'm excited and frightened; my body kind of shutters as loose stools start up again. Friday evening comes. I walk around with Johnny, just trying to describe what I'm feeling to some one who likes me. Words help me keep my grip. He listens softly as we walk in the December darkness.

Later that night I call Bernie at the major seminary. While my heart pumps so loudly that I can hear it, my fingers dial the number. Suddenly I'm hearing Bernie's voice and talking to him like there is nothing out of the ordinary. "Hi Bernie, it's Francis. I wonder if I can talk with you tomorrow?"

"Sure, I'll be over at 3PM. I'll see you then."

I listen to the dial tone for a minute and then hang up. The funny thing is, now that I took the action to call him, I don't feel anxious; instead something real quiet sets in.

Sunday afternoon Bernie enters our rec room, his thumb hooked into the collar of his jacket which hangs nonchalantly over his left shoulder. "How you doing, kid?"

"Oh pretty good Bernie." Without saying anymore we head out the door like it's a prearranged plan.

For years I have been spying on him from a distance; not knowing his insides really, but being finely tuned to every word and gesture; something's different. I can smell a change. The afternoon is mild, but winter is already bringing in chilly dusk. We both are quiet as our feet scrape the sidewalks. I decide I better start. "You see Bernie, I got kind of goofy when I didn't hear from you. I didn't mean to get angry or anything."

Bernie casually takes this in for a minute. "It was a pretty amazing letter." He smiles, but it's a tense smile like he's worried. I've never seen him worried before. He starts up again with some difficulty. "Francis this may be hard for you to understand but everything is different in Chicago. I'm very busy there, but it is not only that. Things aren't working out there as I had imagined." He catches himself and tries to laugh, but his throat chokes it off. He glances at me to see if I noticed. "Francis, sorry for being such a rat and not writing."

He looks sorry and worried like maybe this is part of a string of accidents that he just wants to forget and I'm one of those people who'll punish him for not doing something right. I don't know what to say because I don't want to punish him now. He's afraid and I don't want to make it worse for him. He might live in a world of accidents too. I want to tell him that it's okay to wear his jacket instead of carrying over his shoulder like hero. We all get cold. Instead I say, "Aw, that's all right Bernie. I was just being goofy."

"Thanks Francis."

Then we kind of bury it; the darkness helps. When he does finally put on his jacket he looks all shivery and frail. My sympathy feels like a betrayal. I remember him for a moment the way he was last spring so confident and resourceful, like nothing could shake him. It's about time for me to go back for supper, and besides there's something kind of repetitive in the stuff we're talking about now. I decide to take the lead again. "Well Bernie, thanks a lot for taking the time with me. You've been real kind."

"Well Francis I try my best. This time I'll write, I promise."

"I promise I won't get crazy if you forget."

We shake hands and part. I start walking, but then quickly turn around to watch him disappear.

When I do get back into the seminary, I feel glad for the lights and the card games. I'll think about it all some other time.

When I wake up the next morning I hardly remember what yesterday's drama was all about; but right before philosophy class when most of us are standing outside by the door to our seminary. Bernie drives up and steps out of a car. Everyone starts shaking his hand like he's a departing hero. When it gets to be my turn he whispers to me urgently, "Francis, can I use the bathroom here?"

I nod.

"Where is it?"

I whisper, "Up the stairs and to your right."

He scrambles up the stairs.

Suddenly I know it, I just know it. Bernie has the runs.

There's a pause as people wait for him to come back. I'm the silent keeper of his secret.

In just a few minutes he comes bounding down the stairs having pulled up his swash buckling attitude from around his knees. He nods at me like he's grateful for something or maybe even apologetic and jumps in his car.

The picture of Bernie sitting on the toilet, dumping...I even kind of smell him...is disturbing but still I'm curious about all the changes. Fortunately not much is going on in philosophy class, so I have some time to collect all of the pieces of the last twenty four hours. It's not exactly a feeling or an idea but more like some new place I've stumbled upon again. In this place Bernie and I are made of the same unlucky stuff. Not that we're identical, or even that I know what he's thinking, but that we share some common frailty.

The heaven above me lies empty of the figure that towered in majesty for so long. I ache in some new way that leaves me standing more alone. I know that he will write me, but that's not the point. I don't even feel abandoned or let down; it's something in me that's changed. When Bernie was talking about love that night in May, did he already know about this place where you struggle alone?

I wonder now about Bernie's insides. He's such a hero here. Does that get in his way sometimes? Is that why he looks lonely? I want to pray for him even though I don't know who to pray to anymore. I surround my memories of him with all the tenderness of which I am capable.

Chapter 32

February in Washington is real chancy; shifting without a moment's notice from winter to spring and back again. It's a winter tonight, the cold brightens the stars as Johnny and I slip out of the carefully unlocked door.

Johnny glances over at me. "Wondering if there's a God sure puts a wrench in the works."

We step into the night for a while letting the implications of this statement settle in gently. Walking with Johnny now is the only time I don't feel a nervous dizziness that makes me want to hold on and close my eyes. "Johnny, does it make it harder to decide about the novitiate?"

"No." he becomes very quiet but in a funny closed off sort of way. "The faculty is counting on me. What the heck I suppose I'll go"

I feel my insides open out. "My spiritual director hasn't asked me yet, but of course we don't talk about serious stuff. When I try, he just stares out of that window of his and then asks me how my therapy is going. The God stuff is confusing. In Mary Valley the priests taught us not to think, but just to obey. I tried real hard. Now in Washington the priests say, everything we learned before is childish. Instead there's this magic ladder called Thomistic theology, and God's the last wrung. If you can't climb that one ladder to that last wrung, then there's something wrong with you. Neither place cares a lot about the insides of things, let alone figuring stuff out."

Johnny looks over at me silently; I can tell he's figuring things out with me. "Sometimes I get tired of the way priests throw ideas at us. I'm pretty good about catching them, but I want to decide who to throw the ball to next. It's my ball now, I caught it. I'll use my own intelligence to figure out if I should try to make a double play or get the player out on home base. It's more like a pin ball game here. God or the priests release a metal ball and it bounces from post to post ringing bells and scoring points. We're just the posts that those ideas bang up against and ricochet off in some sort of complex but mechanical way."

I nod. "Ya, it's really strange. The priests talk about freedom of choice and sin, but I feel like I'm chained to a machine that is keeping score. One day I realize I'm losing I can't do anything about it except get more and more nervous. Something wakes up inside but it's all clumsy and scared. I'm in this dark place inside that I wasn't supposed to slip into. But it's not exactly a place that I can even hide in, and it definitely doesn't make things easier here. Johnny, it's not like I tried to find that place, it just happened."

"I don't know where we're going with all of this, Francis." His shoulders kind of hunch together as if it were really cold outside. He stops looking directly at me. "Sometimes after talking with you everything feels pretty wild." He looks ahead now as his shoulders relax a little. He sounds philosophical but not in the way that the priests sound. "I suppose that's why you're good for me. Things come easy me, sometimes I think too easy." He glances at me apologetically.

Chapter 33

Now the priests' staring eyes and the silence settling in around me make me feel foggy; it's like a real unpleasant fogginess. I still try to follow most of the rules, except when I slip out at night with Johnny; but it's getting harder and harder to keep interested in what's going on. That huge sun in the middle of my life, belief in God is fading, and I find I am slipping away, not because I want to, but because the pull that holds my orbit is starting to evaporate. I feel like I'm slowly being released into complete and eerie darkness, like falling, except every direction is down.

One final possibility opens up this last spring. I start getting a crush on Fr. Frank. He's the guy who lives at the major seminary and does a lot of the maintenance here. He has started spending a little more time around here, because he's teaching religion to the freshmen. I'm not sure when my feelings for him actually started. One day I was noticing how relaxed and independent he always looks, and then the next minute I feel this warm excitement that drains into my stomach. It's not like with Bernie of course, but still it's pretty significant. The fact that he's on the faculty gives me a different kind of chance to get to know one of those men who have such power over me. I decide to talk with him about my feelings, picking out an afternoon when he's not as busy with his young friends from another nearby seminary.

It's a grey afternoon in March when everything is cold and dripping wet. I knock on his door. Fr. Frank says, "Come in" like he's all excited about something. I walk in and suddenly he looks impatient or maybe even disappointed.

In the last two years I have become used to being a disappointment so his reaction seems pretty natural. I fumble around a little and then say, "Fr. Frank, there's something I want to talk with you about."

He looks blank for a minute like he's shifting gears that open new possibilities. He looks me up and down in this strange way. "Come in. Lock the door."

Even though it's my fingers closing the lock, the click startles me. I glance at Fr. Frank for reassurance. He's staring at me with an intense look on his face. Again I feel like I am at the top of the tall flimsy pole that is bending in the wind. Air rushes around me and I feel dizzy, afraid like at any moment the pole will break and I'll fall from its height to be smashed on the ground below. I hold on desperately, but know if the pole breaks, it doesn't matter how hard I'm clinging to it. Then I look down. I don't know who or what looks down because I see my body is way below me. Only the flimsy pole connects to me to that body that was myself.

"Sit down."

From above I notice that there are no chairs in the room and watch as my body lowers itself onto the bed.

I feel the heat of his eyes burning into me.

I'm back on ground level now, I feel the softness of the bed under my but…maybe this is just an adventure and before I know it, Fr. Frank and I will be figuring things out.

He nods at me, not so much with reassurance, but like he's prodding me on. He says, "Relax." It's an order.

All those years of obedience have taken their toll. I slump backwards down on the bed, my upper back eventually making contact with the wall against which the bed is positioned, my neck and head held up right by the wall so that I have no choice but to look directly at him. The dizziness has evaporated; I feel I am in a strange field of gravity pulling me, but I don't know what me is anymore. This is my body; this is my blood. But instead of sacrificial bells ringing from an altar I hear this funny whirring sound in my head. I don't really know if I hear or just feel, but the sensation starts gripping my whole body. My inside voice can hardly be heard over the whirring sound. It urgently tells me to be careful. I go ahead anyway. "You see Fr. Frank, I've been learning how it's really okay to let people know my feelings." Yes that's feels better, even though my voice sounds far away. At least I'm doing something. "I wanted to let you know that I have feelings for you. I hope that my telling you…I hope maybe we can become friends."

His eyelids narrow slightly as if he is focusing on something deep inside me.

My body presses deeper into his bed. I squirm a little.

His face looks animated now with a strange tight smile. With some mysterious but determined resolve he rises from his chair, and approaches, kind of wary but not out of fear exactly…more fierce than that. He keeps eye contact.

The whirring sound becomes louder and higher pitched until that is all I can hear.

He sits down next to me.

I feel the bed shake and wonder if he feels me shaking.

He sidles closer to me, pressing his leg against me.

I feel the warmth of his leg. I look away. For a moment I remember when Bernie would touch my shoe or when Don and I would talk regardless of what was happening. The vibrating becomes a little softer. I glance back at Fr. Frank with some hope.

He is staring at me fiercely, eyes that burn through me, through me to something else deeper in my splayed out body. The inside vibration mounts again. I hear something inside whispering one last message from far away, "This isn't like Bernie."

Fr. Frank places his hand on the inside of my leg,

almost like he's listening for something. "Do you have an erection?"

My body reacts on its own…my head nods. The shaking vibrates through the room, I can hardly make my body speak. He doesn't release my eyes from his stare as if he's trying by shear intensity to force his way through some knotty problem that's me. Suddenly frustrated he thrusts himself to his feet and begins pacing. The warmth and pressure from his body evaporates; my body becomes limp. Then with some new resolve he sits down pressing even closer to me. He places his hand on the inside of my leg even higher up, the soft part that no one has even touched before. His eyes push into mine wildly. His voice is slightly hoarse now. "Do you have an erection?"

My teeth are beginning to click together I am shaking so hard. I look away…I think about walking with Johnny at night when we could say whatever we want…I nod to Fr. Frank. And even though my body seems to shake harder by the moment, I know that telling the truth is all that's left.

He focuses on my body in an odd appraising exploration and then stands up again in some final irritation…he's decided something. All wound up in a face as sharp as broken glass he retreats to his desk.

I watch him going a way. I know I have failed some sort of test, but the shaking is quieting. "Have you ever masturbated, Francis?"

He's farther from my body now, behind that big desk.

I feel the probe of his words, but he's not staring at me so intently. He even looks a little bored.

The boredom is reassuring. The shaking is now just a gentle tremor. My body feels stiff and I sit up on the edge of the bed.

"Um, no I haven't; I know most guys have, but I just haven't." I glance at him and look away quickly.

He smiles confidentially, "I believe that masturbating is the only healthy think to do. Why haven't you done it yet?"

He's smiling but his eyes glitter sharply out of his cloud of benevolence. There's menace to his voice. My skinny body squirms below in homely confusion. "I don't know."

His eyes tear at me with frustration and contempt. "What I'd like to do is to strip you naked and make you stand on a chair in the middle of a room, in front of everybody."

The shaking stops now, my self starts crystallizing around the core of some deep guilt never forgotten. I've made a terrible mistake again. Heat brands my face with the sign of shame…another accident…my fault. The world revolves around my corruption…a deadening stillness settles over me that even blocks the scary sexual things that Fr. Hank keeps on droning about.

Then a command of his voice snaps the room awake. "You can go now. Don't tell anybody about this!"

My nightmare focuses and becomes my life; I get

up like he says and unlock the door. My inner voice repeats what Fr. Hank says. "Don't tell anybody about this." There's threat in the voice.

Those words echo like a repeating message…a clue from my inner voice. I unlock the door, not just my fingers, but my whole body, my self walks out that door without looking back…I'm concentrating on the echoing clue. Those words are so familiar…I'm out of the building now walking toward my seminary…the sky is air is gray and foggy and close; it doesn't get in the way of my figuring things out. I take a short cut through the shrubby field with long dry grass growing in it…the sound of my footsteps crunching through the grass…Bud, it's when I was with Bud… what he did…what he did to me…don't tell anybody. I'm out of the field now, walking up the stairs very slowly…I can't believe it, I'm too homely…he wouldn't want something from me. The inner voice says, "Remember."

I don't really believe that voice. What could Fr. Frank want from a skinny pimply kid like me? The rest of my class mates are looking like men, and me…I don't know. But I remember the voice that demanded secrecy. I remember enough to talk the whole thing over with Johnny. I hold it all in until evening when Johnny and I slip out of the door.

"Something really strange happened to me that I just can't quite figure out."

"I'm all ears." He nods, not like the way a priest

nods in the confessional, but like someone who is eager to hear what's going on.

"Well this afternoon I decided to tell Fr. Frank that I have feelings for him, kind of like with Bernie."

"Yes…Francis." He looks a little tense, but he's still there.

"Well I get in the door and he asks me to lock it. Then he sits next to me and puts his hand on my leg and asks me if I have an erection…twice he did that."

"What the heck!"

"Then for about an hour he talks to me about masturbation and how he wants to stand me on a chair naked in front of everybody. Finally he tells me to leave and not tell what happened."

Johnny is puzzling it out. "I wonder what he was doing; it doesn't make sense. Has he gone crazy or something?"

"What I was wondering…when I was real young, a neighbor did sexual things to me. I know it doesn't make sense, but I wonder if there is a connection to that?"

Johnny shakes his head as if this quandary is beyond his figuring out skills. "I don't know, but he sure was doing something strange. You won't go up to see him anymore, will you Francis?"

"No, I feel sick to my stomach even when I think about him."

Then we just keep walking and talking about other thinks like so many other times in the seminary.

The next morning a single bird decided it was

time and woke up the whole chattering sky. My eyes are wide open; it's still gray outside. As the morning commotion sifts through the window, I realize it's Saturday morning. There is so little privacy in the seminary, but this moment seems like something just meant for me.

I've always liked Saturday mornings…only the drowsy sound of a barking dog in the distance reminds me of a world beyond this moment. It's not that I'm optimistic about the future; it's just that the future is at a distance. I hear a steady voice inside me gently whisper, "It's time to go." The whisper echoes louder than that far off future. In my sleep some pieces have settled into place. Like some one has collected the scenes of my life in the seminary and put them in a box which they shook and dumped out. The miracle is that they form a picture, and looking at the picture, I Francis Meyers don't want to stay at the seminary for the rest of my life…I just don't want to. I don't know what I can do away from here, but…

The sound of a flushing toilet in the next room shatters the possibilities of silence. The bustle of a seminary morning begins. My fellow seminarians are stirring: beds creaking, the sound of faucets turning on…doors opening, footsteps. The quiet part of Saturday morning is over. My body tightens…what would I do out in the world…there's nothing I want to do…the seminary is my last resort. I couldn't exist outside of here.

My body starts going through the motions of

getting up, so automatic, so easy. Like some reprieve I come up with an idea…I'll ask for a year's leave. Guys here do that periodically. That way I can get away for a little while and regroup without saying goodbye. Maybe what happened with Fr. Frank wasn't so bad after all. If I get away for just a little while maybe all the things I have been wondering about these past two years will fade. I'll wake one morning, and life in the priesthood will start again…this is just kind of a stage I'm going through. My inside voice is very quiet. It simply says, "Yes you need to get away."

I mention to Johnny that I might not be around here for a next year, not that I'm going away forever or anything like that. He doesn't seem surprised, but I think I see his eyes go sad for a moment. Then he smiles easy going and says, "Francis you go ahead and do whatever you need to do." Neither of us talk about my leaving after that.

Now I just need to talk with the superior, Fr. Marquand, to get this year's leave thing all set up. I've never spoken with him much before; I guess we had a bad start and never quite got over that. When I step into his room, I see he's concentrating on some papers lying in front of him. He's frowning like there's something terribly wrong with whatever he's looking at. He motions me to sit down using that hand with missing fingers and continues for a few moments to be angry at those papers in front of him. I wonder about those fingers and the terrible things that can happen to people. The way he never talks about them I wonder if he had to forget.

He snaps his head up at me like he has been called to attention. I sit up a little straighter and try to look into those bright, empty eyes.

"Father, I've been thinking about this a lot. I'd like a year's leave from the seminary."

His face doesn't register anything except that his mouth starts moving. "The faculty has been very concerned about you. We have watched your behavior very closely. In most of your classes, especially theology, you look distracted. There are indications that something is wrong with you. As you know we asked you to see a therapist last year. Your behavior has not improved. You will have your leave, but you can only come back if two psychiatrists indicate that your mental health is satisfactory, up to par, so to speak." His dolls eyes focus on me.

The room spins tumbling me, but something foggy prevents me from knowing where I am. I'm too sleepy now to figure out what's happening. I hardly care that he's staring at me.

"Do you understand?"

"Yes Father." But I don't really. For a moment pictures of Johnny, Bernie, Don, card games, figuring things out, my future all slip by inside my head, slip by like dreams inside my head that even memory can hardly grasp. There's something wrong with me, now everybody knows it. Silence settles in, not the silent night of Christmas, but the silence of pointless dread. Like no matter how hard I try to escape, the future just pounces on me and tears me apart. This has nothing to do with figuring things out…it has to do with something more inevitable.

He's smiling now, like my distant silence confirms the correctness of his diagnosis. What price does he pay for being right like that? His eyes return to the papers on his desk and I turn and leave automatically.

While I think I'm growing, my life is really eroding from underneath me. Something about the way I'm put together is wrong. That voice inside…I don't want to listen to that voice inside. It taunts me with the possibilities of life unwinding and then leaves me torn apart and swallowed up by dread.

I mention something about the psychiatrists to Johnny; he's puzzled, but is now thinking about his own separate future in the novitiate. He decided to go. He asks me to spend a week with him and his family at the end of school. I say yes. I tell Don about asking for a year's leave, but there's this little complication about being crazy. He says he looks forward to my coming back. I write Bernie and mention about the leave of absence but nothing more.

In the remaining few weeks, Gene and Tim talk a lot about next year; how wonderful it will be. Silence rings around me so widely that farewells cannot get through.

Tim dives into his future with only a brief, nervous glance in my direction. Gene, more knowing and skilled, confidently severs the cord of our relationship quickly, perhaps out of mercy. With Mario, it's not so simple. He's decided to quit the seminary and explore that land of hopes that he and Bonnie have been writing about. Still, the amputation pains him too much to say goodbye to anyone.

Now to the last we maintain vague, seminary friendliness.

I call my parents and reassuringly tell them about the slight alteration in my plans, "only a year, you know." They hesitate to ask questions.

Chapter 34

Everything is set for the last night. During supper Fr. Marquand announces how proud he is of the seminarians going on to the novitiate. We applaud. The meal ends. I pack. Evening darkens. Don knocks on my bedroom door.

"Francis I wanted to be sure to see you before you left. Not to say goodbye, because I know, you'll be back. We'll go swimming again and talk about God. I'll fill you in on what's happened while you were gone."

"Sure Don."

"Hey, let's go for a walk?"

"Thanks Don, but I've got all this packing to do… maybe when I come back."

And then we just stand there, Don blinking a lot like he's holding something back that mustn't get through.

"Let me give you a hug, I won't be seeing you for a while."

For the first time in my life, I rest just for a second

in the arms of a man. Then I tear myself away, so as not to embarrass him.

"See you Don."

"See you Francis."

Another step, another step, another step, until the world out of which I live, disappears.

Johnny and I spend the week in Richland, almost like so many other weeks; walking and talking a lot, wondering about God and the world; me a little dramatic, he a little flat.

Then one morning early, he drives me to the Greyhound bus station in Richland. I think of all kinds of eloquent things I want to say about my feelings for him, but I know there's no time; besides he likes things simple and calm.

We shake hands, say goodbye, and I leave Johnny forever in a bus station in Richland West Virginia on a cloudy Saturday morning at exactly 8:30AM.

Chapter 35

I take the bus from Richland. I change busses in Chicago. I take Darryl's phone number out of my wallet, unfold it, look at it for a moment, and throw it in a trash can in the bus depot. Like I said before that first trip to the seminary just beyond the brink of childhood; I never was brave.

Besides, nothing matters anyway.

The bus drives through Wisconsin now. The stops are backwards; each town bringing me closer to a place I thought I had escaped. Once upon a time I was afraid to loose that pale blue suitcase enclosing all the possessions of childhood. Now that stubborn companion accompanies me, unbidden, the contents of a failed, preposterous life enclosed.

A world of God, order, learning, love, flattens to vague memory. I already miss it, my old world; but I do kind of understand that things are not as simple as they seem…I'm not as simple either. The wheels set in motion, the wheels I thought I had evaded, grind on again toward the future. Perhaps during these six years of the seminary those gears never really stopped; all along they were moving unheard. That dark inner spring draws me.

Dad picks me up at the bus station. His hair is grayer, but he wears that same expression of embarrassed sadness; I'm not angry at him now. I know something about disappointment. Besides a cloudy, plastic sheet separates me from the world.

I meet my mother in the kitchen. We both know that there are no more new worlds she can introduce me to. We reassure each other.

And yes I wrote Bernie. We exchanged greetings twice that year. In the last letter he ever wrote me, he mentioned that he was quitting the seminary.

On one of those Saturday mornings when things seemed a little clearer, I realized that I didn't want to spend my life revolving around his distant star…not so much out of personal hope, just fatigue. I wrote a letter thanking him for his kindness and sent it off. I never heard from him again, but at least I said sort of a goodbye. Sometimes in my dreams I still see him running ahead, always at a distance; try as I may, I can never quite reach him.

I never even considered returning to the seminary, although it really wasn't an option. I suppose options imply choices and choices seem like privileges for the fortunate.

Don and I wrote several times. He was ordained and started teaching in Chicago. After a hiatus of two years, I wrote him again. I was between things and asked him if I could hitch hike over to visit him. I mentioned about being gay. He wrote a cool letter back; not mean or anything, just cool. I decided not to go.

Johnny quit the seminary a year after I did. We wrote each other for a few years. I even asked him if he wanted to go to San Francisco with me. He thanked me for the invitation, but said that he was going to graduate school. Once every five years or so, I called him just to check up. He was always friendly, but pretty busy with his own life. In my last move, I think I lost his phone number. My last move…

Chapter 36

Through negligible slits Francis spied out at the unfamiliar shore upon which he had been cast, his solitary bedroom, lights still on from the night before, a night of dreams. Slowly the confines of the familiar apartment began asserting their demands: the bright overhead light he should have been turned off, the plants drying up in the overheated room… he didn't know how to turn the radiator down, his clothes, even his shoes were still on. His usual fears scraped in rhythm to the sound of his clock on the dresser: things to be done, things to be done, things to be done.

Even with all the commotion of his regrets, he thought he heard a familiar little voice from inside whisper, "Sorrow." He stared out. There is something so quiet about sorrow; he wondered about that, kind of a resting place, no escape, but no fear.

He suddenly became aware of the coolness around his eyes, wetness. Irritated, he tried to blink it away.

Again the voice whispered, "Sorrow."

He whispered, "Sorrow."

He took his clothes off. Just as his eyes began closing again he found himself figuring things out, thinking. "Sorrow…feels kind of open, almost gentle, like home, like something you can't lose because everything is gone anyway, home." That wisp of amazement disappeared into sleep.

Chapter 37

There was a knock at the door.

"Oh my God, I over slept!" Francis jumped up, threw on his cloths and scrambled to the living room, clicking shoe laces trailing. He grasped the knob and swung the door open; April sunlight softly exploded in his eyes; Chris stood revealed in the doorway.

"Chris, I'm sorry. I don't know what got into me. I just slept so soundly. Sorry, sorry I'm not ready."

"That's all right. I was a little early anyway. I'll sit down here and wait for you to finish."

Francis walked back to the bedroom smiling. If you asked him right then if he was happy, he would probably pause for a few seconds before remembering that vague fear of accidents...that pause, an opening, a grace, another kind of accident.

After hardly enough time Francis rushed back into the living room, Chris sat upright next to the window like some sentinel of the morning. "I'm already Chris, I'm already. Let's go."

Chris took a slow look at his brother, stood up very seriously and nodded. "Well, let's get going."

Chris led the way, his gait, determined but shuffling slightly. The anti-psychotic drugs that he had been taking for years had left a mark.

Frances closed the door, locking it, and snuck in a few quick steps to catch up with his brother. April air nestled against them as the frozen ground began sweating in patches wherever the rays of Saturday sun touched. Bird calls saturated the world with gentle possibility. Francis turned to Chris. "Have you gone fishing yet?"

Chris chewed on that for a moment. "Well Francis, the ice has started to break up but not enough yet, soon, soon."

Chris's pace picked up as they approached a busy intersection; the untidy sounds of an inner city avenue closed in. There at the corner stood a shiny restaurant; one of those chain restaurants where waitresses wear uniforms and name tags and are trained in by nervous young men beginning to go bald.

Chris in the lead, the brothers stepped through the threshold. A familiar waitress glanced at them over the muzak bringing coffee and a moment of recognition. For the next forty five minutes Francis and Chris sat, occasionally nodding and exchanging words in simultaneous satisfaction.

"How are you doing today, Francis?"

"Oh pretty well, I mean, I slept really soundly last night. The strange thing was, before I went to sleep I just kept remembering things, things I haven't thought about for a long time."

"Was it all right?" Chris looked worried and then smoothed that out with reassurance.

"Oh sure, some sad things, but somehow..." Frances's voice faded into figuring out. Chris nodded over his coffee.

They sat, two graying people together for an overly long time. But if you too have had your journeys home, you'll understand that it's not desolation that brings them to this spot every week but amazement, amazement with all the ways we struggle to escape as life unwinds. Almost accidentally, and in fits and starts, that struggle can light something fierce in a soul, something that feels and learns.

Coffee over, they examined the familiar mystery of the check and decided once again to split it. Francis placed a tip on the table and gave a goodbye smile to the waitress.

She said, "Take care of yourself, honey."

The brothers walked through the shiny glass door stepping out to a world surprised into spring. Green buds sneaked through the newly soft ground that filled the air with the sweet, peppery splendor of last fall's decay.

"Hey Chris, do you remember that story you wrote a long time ago about that girl with the rainbow eyes?"

"Can't say as I do. You sure have a good memory for things like that."

"Chris, do you want to go for breakfast next week?"

"Sure Francis."
"I'm glad your home."

****

Now home isn't exactly a place. It's wherever we keep being sent back to, sent back by the limits of our imagination longing to finally break open, turning a maze into a tumble of wonder; a sometimes reluctant journey but true, leading not so much to a destination but to a beginning.